Starlet

Starlet

by Randi Reisfeld

Hyperion
New York

Text copyright © 2007 by Randi Reisfeld

First edition

1 3 5 7 9 10 8 6 4 2

Printed in the United States of America

This book is set in ITC Century Light.

ISBN-13: 978-14231-0501-5

ISBN-10: 1-4231-0501-X

Visit www.hyperionteens.com

Starlet

Chapter One

"... I'd Like to Thank My Massage Artiste ..."

Jacey Chandliss surrendered herself to the powerful hands of a complete stranger. Except for a heated bath towel draped across her tush, Hollywood's newly minted It girl was buck naked, stretched across a cushy massage table, belly down on a thick pile of soft, gazillion-ply sheets.

For the first time in weeks, she was relaxed, as a guy she had only just met rubbed a mixture of essential oils and honey into her bare back. His name was Paolo, and he pressed his thumbs down gently in circular motions around and beneath her shoulder blades. His magic fingers kneaded her neck, scalp, arms, and legs.

"How does that feel, Miss Chandliss?" Paolo asked.

"Best massage I've ever had," Jacey murmured. *Only one I've ever had*, she thought.

"Excellent! I'm honored to be your massage artiste." He pronounced it *ar-teeste*.

Jacey stifled a giggle. She was seventeen years old and had never been away from home without her parents before, and Paolo was treating her like royalty.

The massage artiste increased the pressure slightly, working in small circles on her lower back. "All the stars come here to Torrey Pines spa—Beyoncé and Madonna. But you're the one everyone is most excited about."

"Beyoncé comes here? And you're excited about me? You're joking." She twisted her neck to look up at him. They were stars, icons. All she'd ever done was win top prize in a new reality TV show.

"I'm serious!" the chiseled-jawed dye-guy insisted. "When *Generation Next* was on TV, the staff was obsessed with it. We never missed a week. We voted for you over and over again!"

"So you guys helped me win—I totally owe you!" Sweet memories poured over her as Paolo slathered a warmed honey mixture onto her calves. The *Generation Next* TV competition had ended six months earlier; her prize for winning had been a part in a big Hollywood movie and an amazing new life that included free weekends at luxurious spas like this.

"You deserved to win!" Paolo proclaimed. "You were the best looking—and the best actress, the most talented. A lethal combination in showbiz."

"That's so sweet of you to say."

"Oh! But it's true. I really mean it."

Half-credit, Jacey thought. Best looking? Not in *her* mirror. True, the show's producers had dubbed her "the beauty," but all she saw were glaring flaws. Her shiny waves of copper-colored hair framed a too-round face, while her startling, ocean-colored eyes were set in a too-pale complexion, and her bee-stung lips made her look pouty when she wasn't smiling. When she did crack a grin, it was usually megawatt, and her deep double dimples staged a complete takeover of her face.

Had she been the best actress on the show? Hard to say. She'd been doing it all her life—besides school plays and community theater, she was always acting cool and confident when she felt sweaty and insecure, acting surprised when she knew all along what was going to happen, acting as if things didn't matter when they totally did. Acting came as naturally to her as breathing. And it was just as necessary.

Her dream was to become a professional actress, a movie star.

Her reality was a thoroughly ordinary, obscure, day-to-day life: school, homework, friends, boyfriend, family, nice suburban neighborhood. She was not complaining, but what were the odds of making the dream come true? It was a long shot at best.

Jacey Lyn Chandliss, only child of autoworker Cecile and long-gone bio-dad Jacob, had no connections, no route from Bloomfield Hills, Michigan, to Beverly Hills, California. It wasn't as if Hollywood was gonna come knocking at her door.

Until the day it did.

Generation Next: The Search for America's Top Young Actor was holding auditions in cities all across the USA, including Detroit, Michigan. That stop on the Gen Next Audition Express was where it had all started.

The show, set up just like *American Idol*, became just as wildly popular. Instead of singing, contestants were judged on their acting ability. Each week, they acted out scenes from popular movies or TV shows, performing solo or opposite other contestants.

A panel of judges, including a casting agent, acting teacher, and movie director, evaluated the performances. As on *American Idol*, the audience voted contestants off—or, in Jacey's case, on, week after week.

She'd won a big part in a major motion picture called

Four Sisters, which was an update of the classic *Little Women*. If a guy had won *Generation Next*, he'd have played the lead male role.

Paolo was one of the millions who'd voted to see Jacey win the part. The massage guy now wanted in on the behind-the-scenes dish.

"Do you mind if I ask you some questions about the way it really worked?" Paolo continued to stroke the warm honey and floral oils into her back, arms, and shoulders.

"Go for it," Jacey said encouragingly.

"Okay, so, did you guys really choose the scenes you acted out? Or did they give them to you?"

"Some weeks you brought in your scene. Other weeks, you'd come in and they'd give you the lines, just before you went on live TV. It's called a cold reading. No rehearsal."

"Really?" Paolo acted shocked. "That's what they told the viewers, but I didn't think it was true."

"That part was!" Jacey remembered the week they'd given her a scene from *Macbeth*. She'd never read the play, but had had less than ten minutes to interpret a Lady Macbeth soliloquy.

"Yeeesh. That must have been hard!"

"It was!" She'd gotten her lowest score that week.

"What about that scene you did from *Clueless*, where Cher gets mugged and all she's worried about is getting her designer dress dirty? I pissed in my pants when you did that one, the way you whined, 'It's an *Alàia!*'"

That had been the most fun scene Jacey had performed. It was a ridiculous situation; yet the character was really sincere. The *Gen Next* audience loved her interpretation.

"Oh, but in the season finale, the way they dragged it out before announcing the winner." Paolo clutched his throat. "We were totally dying here. I can't imagine how you must have felt."

"Like vomiting," Jacey admitted. "It was all I could do to keep my stomach from erupting."

Paolo laughed heartily. "Me, too!"

That was a scene that played over and over again in her head like a loop. Sean Brean, the show's announcer, was a chicly shaggy-haired graduate of the Ryan Seacrest School of Generic Hosts. He dragged out every last ounce of tension. "So, who has it come down to, America? Who have you chosen as the winner of *Generation Next: The Search for America's Top Young Actor?*"

No way was he gonna simply announce the winner. Torturously, Sean backpedaled: "Let's go over the three finalists one last time. It's come down to the drama queen, the perky comic, and the beauty. Who have you picked?

Angela Harris—eighteen, dark, and willowy, was the

drama queen. Her specialty was heart-wrenching death scenes; no matter what part she acted out, she wore black. New York City loved her!

Sean droned on, "America, you gave Angie the most points when she enacted the death scene from *Romeo and Juliet*, but the fewest when she warbled 'Smelly Cat' as Phoebe on *Friends*. So how did it add up in the end?"

On cue, Angie's Angels, as her cheering section was called, did a routine that included flapping their "wings" while clapping.

"Or," Sean continued when the Angie applause died down, "have you chosen Carlin?"

Carlin McClusky, the "ditzy comic of Cleveland" had tickled her way into audiences' hearts. Like a clumsy puppy, Carlin goofed up all the time. She had the mushy-hearts vote locked. Carlin's Crew did a sort of bump-and-grind cheer as Sean reminded the audience, "Carlin charmed you as Elle Woods in *Legally Blonde*, but alarmed you as Elizabeth in *Pride and Prejudice*."

"And now we come to Jacey." Sean affected a serious tone. "Audience, you rooted for the beauty's version of Cher in *Clueless*, but you hooted at her interpretation of Lady Macbeth."

Jacey's posse, including her cousin Ivy; best friends, Desiree and Dash; boyfriend, Logan; and her parents and aunt, gave her a standing ovation, stamping their feet while applauding wildly.

Jacey tensed up remembering it.

Finally, Sean had said, "And the winner of *Generation Next* . . ."

He paused, and pointed at the camera. ". . . Will be announced after the break! Stay right where you are, America!"

"That was so annoying, how they made us all wait until after the commercial!" Paolo exclaimed, wrapping her in the cool linen sheets. "It was maddening for us viewers. I can't imagine what it was like for you. Unless . . ." He was fishing for gossip. ". . . You knew ahead of time which one it would be . . ."

"I'm not that great an actress!" Jacey said. "That fear and dread you saw was the real deal, jelly legs and all."

She recalled the way the commercial break had ended, and how the suspense level had risen.

"I know you've all been waiting on pins and needles. So . . ." Sean had rubbed his hands together. "We won't make you wait a moment longer. The title of America's Top Young Actor goes to . . ."

Jacey had been crazy, dizzy—sweaty in places she didn't want to think about, but was sure everyone could see! *Say my name, say my name.* . . . The classic

Destiny's Child song had danced through her brain, while her heart had beat so loud she was sure the others on stage could hear it.

"The performer who'll star in *Four Sisters* is . . ."

When her name was announced, she couldn't believe it. She was being hugged by Carlin and Angela, and there was confetti everywhere.

The moment she'd been crowned America's Top Young Actress, Jacey's life had gone from "Whoo-hoo, you *won!*" to "What the f***? I *won?*"

Jacey and her mom had crisscrossed the country at least four times so that she could appear on national and local TV news and entertainment shows, to promote *Generation Next* and to thank the millions who had voted for her. She answered the same questions over and over again ("How did it feel when they called your name?" "How does it feel to be so popular, an instant starlet?"), signed countless autographs, posed for pictures, and smiled until she thought her face would break in half.

It was weird that all those famous TV reporters and hosts were so nice to her, so interested in her. They made her feel comfortable, special. Professional hairdressers and makeup artists fawned over her, getting her camera ready. *A girl could get used to all the pampering,* she texted her friends.

Jacey's big win netted her something else every young actress needs: an agent! And hers had the best Hollywood name—Cinnamon T. Jones. The *T* probably stood for 'tude, because Cinnamon was swathed in Hollywood attitude. In a good way.

She talks really fast! Everything is urgent! Jacey texted Ivy, Dash, and Desi. *Every sentence ends with FABULOUS!*

By the time Jacey got back to school, she'd had enough of being interviewed and photographed. She was "smiled" and "fabulous-ed!" out. It was hard catching up with the rest of her senior class, but, with the help of teachers, parents, and friends, she did it.

The best part of being home and just Jacey again was reconnecting with Logan Finnerty.

Officially "the boyfriend," for a period going on two years, Logan, star of the basketball team, *and* probable valedictorian, welcomed her back with delicious kisses. They were Jacey and Logan again: their own personal J.Lo.

That was the upside of getting back to life as she'd known it.

It wasn't destined to last very long.

Because of the publicity swirling around her, the schedule for *Four Sisters* was moved up. It was to be filmed smack in the middle of the school year! Jacey had no idea how she was going to pull it off, but the geography gods were with her. As it turned out, *Four Sisters*'s location shoot was to be in Chicago, less than an hour away by plane from Detroit. Which made it possible to go home on weekends and during breaks. With the help of a tutor, she pulled her usual Bs, with a sprinkling of Cs. Not too shabby. And when combined with all she had learned from being in her first real movie, it was probably the best education she'd ever had.

The trio of famous actresses who starred along with her, Julia Barton, Kate Summers, and Sierra Tucson, had all helped her.

After *Four Sisters* wrapped, Jacey returned to high school, this time fully expecting to "stay put for a while," as her mom, Cece, and stepdad, Larry, had put it teasingly. To them, "a while" meant until graduation. Then she could start college as a film major.

She hadn't been back in Mrs. Ehrlich's homeroom for more than a couple of weeks when Cinnamon paged her. Jacey dashed to the principal's office to take the call.

"Fabulous news! *Four Sisters* is going to open on May fifteenth. You'll come out to Los Angeles now, and stay for the summer."

Now? Jacey's mind raced. April was SATs. May was

Wicked, the big musical production at school. May was . . . just before June: graduation and prom.

"Perfect!" Cinnamon went into auto-agent mode. "You'll do press, promotions, publicity, and, let's see, we'll get you booked into a Dodgers baseball game."

"Why?" Jacey was borderline alarmed.

"To throw out the first ball. It'll be a photo op. *People* magazine will use it; so will *US Weekly*."

Jacey's stomach somersaulted. Questions formed, but the only one that made it out was, "Can I call you back? I'm . . . in the principal's office, and everyone's staring at me."

"Then, toss your head, and shoot them that high-beam smile of yours. And call me back the instant you can!"

Jacey did not follow those directions. When the final bell rang, she whipped out her cell phone and texted Logan. *Meet me now? Important.*

B-ball practice. After? came the reply.

She decided to wait around. Heading toward the basketball courts, she ran into Dash, her next-door neighbor and closest male confidant—and shanghaied him into waiting with her for Logan. Curly-haired, serious Dash could tell that Jacey had news. "Spill," he commanded, settling next to her in the bleachers.

She told him all—including her anxiety about leaving

for California so soon.

"And you wouldn't go to Hollywood for the summer. . . . Why, exactly? Where's the downside?" Dash asked.

"It's . . ." she faltered.

"Let's see. A freebie summer spent kicking up your heels in Hollywood, hobnobbing with the stars, partying in the thick of showbiz, deciding on your next movie . . . Or . . ." He paused to mime balancing a scale. "A summer spent in Bloomfield Hills, Michigan, doing . . . ? What *was* it you were gonna do here?"

She frowned, hating it when Dash was right. Which was pretty much always.

"If I went—*big* if—who'd come with?" she asked. "It's not like my parents can just take off four months of work." She might have added that her mom had just found out that she was pregnant. But the pregnancy was high risk, and Jacey wasn't supposed to tell anyone yet.

Dash considered. "I would. I would come with you."

"Really? This is the between-high-school-and-college summer—don't you have some big, important internship or something?"

"You mean the one at Borders corporate headquarters in Ann Arbor? Three months in a cubicle, facing a computer screen all day? That one?"

She laughed. "Not really looking forward to it, huh?"

"If I could be hangin' in Hollywood, with you? It kinda pales. And you know what? I bet Desi would come; and what's Ivy doing this summer, now that she's graduated college? It's not like she has a career. Or even a job."

"The whole posse," Jacey mused. "Except—"

"Speak. What's to keep you here?"

Jacey motioned toward the court, where Logan, wearing shorts and a b-ball tank top—all lean, sinewy, and graceful—sank a basket. Leaving him for the entire summer was a nervous-making idea. They'd gone through a rough patch when she was on the West Coast for *Generation Next*; there'd been misunderstandings and missed communication even when she'd been in Chicago filming *Four Sisters*.

When she and Logan were together, they were good. Better than good. But the long-distance thing?

Jacey chewed her fingernails, sensing Dash staring at her.

"This is what you've always wanted, Jacey. Why put the brakes on now?"

"So, by 'this,' do you mean Hollywood, or Logan?"

"Logan will be here when you get back."

"And if he's not?"

The buzzer sounded, and a sweaty, knobby-kneed Logan, so cute with a towel around his neck—what girl wouldn't want him?—bounded up to them. "Hey, J. Hey, D. I'm running to the shower. Be right back."

A short while later, Logan pulled the Pontiac Sunbird out of the student parking lot.

"You're proud of me, right?" Jacey asked Logan.

Stopping for a red light, he eyed her quizzically. "What?"

"I mean, with . . . all that's happened? Winning the show, making the movie?"

He gave her a look she couldn't interpret. Bewilderment? Confusion? Suspicion? Annoyance? And an answer that revealed nothing: "Why wouldn't I be proud of you? Our whole town is."

Our town, Jacey thought. Like *that* mattered. "I care about you. I care about us."

The light changed and Logan hit the gas. "What am I missing here, Jacey? You're my girl. Of course I'm proud of you! I'll be first in line when *Four Sisters* opens." He steered the car into her cul-de-sac and threw it into park. "Why are you acting all insecure?" He put his arm around her.

Jacey's cell phone rang. The ring tone was "Hooray for Hollywood," the one she'd programmed for Cinnamon. Jacey tried to wriggle away from Logan, but just then he whispered in her ear, in a way that made her tingly all over. "You can call whoever it is right back."

"I kinda have to take this, Logan. Give me one sec."

Cinnamon, off and running, took many secs. "I've rented you an apartment; it's temporary, but it'll do for the summer. Your lease starts April first. Don't thank me!"

"Cinn—I haven't decided yet," Jacey stammered.

Logan gave up trying for a romantic moment. He killed the engine, got out of the car, came around to her side, and helped her out. Jacey put one finger in the air, signaling him to hang on, but Logan, having figured out who she was on the phone with, kissed the top of her head and murmured, "I love you, Jacey." Then he slid back into the driver's seat and turned the engine back on.

"*Four Sisters* is a huge movie," Cinnamon blathered on. "We need you here to get ready for the gala premiere. It's going to be fabulous!"

Jacey watched Logan drive away. Into the phone, she said, "*Four Sisters* comes out in May. Why would I need to stay until September?"

"Why? To establish yourself, to meet and greet, to read scripts, to decide on your next project, to take meetings! That's what actors do, Jacey."

On April 10, Jacey left for Hollywood. Her parents had been skeptical about letting her go, but when her friends stepped up—Dash, Desi, and Ivy—they gave her their blessing. Everything was settled with school, and Jacey had taken her finals and SATs early.

During their first whirlwind week in L.A., Jacey and her pals had been treated to some serious freebies: front-row seats at a Kanye West concert, where Desi dived into the mosh pit; an all-access backstage pass to a Sheryl Crow concert; free screenings of upcoming summer blockbusters; and VIP passes to clubs-you-read-about-in-magazines and restaurants-so-chic-you-don't!

The weekend at the luxurious Torrey Pines spa near San Diego was another perk. The four of them got massaged, wrapped, waxed, exfoliated, oiled, masked, scented, and salt-, seaweed-, and/or grape seed–scrubbed until their skin either glowed in the dark or simply fell off.

With one final squeeze of her shoulders, Paolo ended her session.

"Thank you," Jacey said, *so* not wanting to get up from the table. Every muscle in her body was relaxed.

She heard Desi giggle and Ivy snort. Grabbing her robe, she went outside her cabana and saw her three friends hanging out by the pool. Dash spied her first and rushed over to her.

"Paris is here!" he exclaimed. "How cool is that?"

"Her bodyguard told me about a party." Desi's eyes

sparkled excitedly. "Please, please, pretty please, can we go? When will we ever get to party with Paris?"

"We can't," Ivy told them. "Jacey has the *Seventeen* magazine cover shoot tomorrow. And—don't even think of it—where she goes, so do we."

"We're the entourage—she's the starlet."

Jacey Exposed!

What's up, Jacey Chandliss fans? You don't know me, but I know *her*. Who am I? That's for me to know—and Jacey to find out. Maybe.

She's on her wild Hollywood ride, and this is your all-access pass to come along! I'll be your chatty fly on the wall. Everything she does, everyone she meets, every time there's news, I'll be bloggin' it right here!

Like what? Like how 'bout right now, as you're reading this, she's chillin' at the most exclusive, luxurious, celebrity-studded spa in all the land—the place where J.Lo, Scarlett, Madonna, and Beyoncé go to get pampered. And how ya like these apples? Those stars pay. Jacey (and her entourage!) are there for free—a little "thank you" perk from her grateful *Generation Next* bosses.

Speaking of free, why am I providing this service gratis? Because you voted her to stardom. You deserve to know.

And because I can.

Chapter Two

Shoot Me Now

Jacey stared into the mirror.

Bozo the Clown stared back.

Her lips, naturally full, had been painted cherry red; her cheeks glared like scarlet headlights on high beam. Her eyebrows, brushed and penciled, bore a striking resemblance to the golden arches of McDonald's. If someone squeezed her nose, would it honk?

What a difference a day makes! Yesterday, she'd been at Torrey Pines spa, feeling relaxed and gorgeous. Today, she was in the dressing room of the *Seventeen* photo studio, feeling like Barnum & Bailey bait.

Her hair was its own special disaster. Her shoulder-length wavy tresses had been bound—and gagged—wound

in with extensions, then cinched into . . . tufts of thick pig-
tails?

Jacey was too horrified to speak.

"Delicious!" the *Seventeen* stylist, Aleta Baggins, said
as she swept into the dressing room clapping her hands
delightedly. "Jacey, you look yummy enough to eat—
wholesome as carb-free apple pie!"

"Are you . . . sure? I feel a little . . ." She hesitated.
". . . Clownish."

Aleta, a big woman, laughed heartily. "We gave you a
dewy flush—candy-colored, flushed cheeks are *hot!*"

Maybe this look *was* in, but she was definitely not
okay with it. Especially not for her first magazine cover.

"Trust me on this, honey, you put yourself in my hands.
You'll be thanking me a year from now!" Aleta proudly held
up the outfit she'd brought in for Jacey to wear.

It wasn't the skinny black jeans Jacey objected to
(though she couldn't imagine being able to zip them). It
wasn't even the toe-cleavage sandals. It was the—how to
put this?—milkmaid top. A sheer, white-lace, frothy thing
with short, puffy sleeves and a thick raspberry ribbon
across the bust. She already saw herself in the When Bad
Clothes Happen to Good People column.

"I scored you a Dolce & Gabbana top!" Aleta crowed.

"Do I have to wear it?" Jacey whined.

Aleta arched her own overdone eyebrows. "What do you mean, darling? You'll look—"

"Like 'Heidi Does the Circus'?"

Aleta's smile faded. Turning her back on Jacey, she hung the offensive outfit on the coat hook. "Wholesome— that's the image I was told we were going for with you. This is my interpretation of it. I'm sorry if you have a problem with that."

Jacey reached out and touched Aleta's arm. "I'm really sorry, I didn't mean to criticize. . . ." She faltered. "It's not personal, it's . . ." She trailed off again.

"Put the outfit on. We'll see when you come out of the dressing room."

"I'll look . . ."

Aleta was already down the hall before Jacey could say more.

Jacey, Ivy, Dash, and Desi had arrived earlier that morning at the photo studio. It was a bright, cavernous space chock-full of lights, umbrellas, backdrops, props, and, best of all, rows and rows of killer outfits.

"I'm in haute couture heaven!" Ivy had gushed, rushing over to the racks. "This is like being at A/X Armani with no limits! I'm *so* picking some looks for you." She'd begun pulling out tops, shrugs, jeans, and belts when the

Seventeen staff walked in—and, in the nicest of all possible ways—ended *that* frivolity.

Aleta, large 'n' in charge, had laid down the rules: "You can't choose, you can't keep, and you can't veto—anything. Don't even ask about doing your own hair and makeup: that's what we're here for."

"We" consisted of Aleta, a photographer with two assistants, a makeup artist, a hairstylist, and their assistants, the editorial director of the magazine, and a reporter, who'd be interviewing Jacey later.

The posse? Outgunned.

Ivy, Desi, and Dash settled for hanging on the couch, helping themselves to the catered breakfast: muffins, bagels, fresh fruit, yogurt, granola, teas, lattes, and cappuccinos. Meanwhile, Jacey had been shuttled into the hair and makeup rooms. It had taken thirty-one makeup brushes of all sizes and shapes; a rainbow of shadows, blushes, and glosses; and irons, both curling and flat—all to achieve this hideous result.

When Aleta returned to the dressing room, she tried to reassure Jacey. "You look adorable," she purred. "Just like America's sweetheart should. Here, you'll pose holding this." She handed her a single, perfect daisy.

Jacey sneezed.

"Come," Aleta urged. "Your agent has arrived, along with your publicist—let's see what they think."

More important were her friends' opinions. *They'd* be honest.

Okay, maybe too honest.

Desi, who'd been drinking from a bottle of iced tea, tried to swallow first, but didn't make it. She sprayed the room, hooting. "You glow in the dark!"

Ivy cocked her head. "She looks . . . feverish."

Dash folded his arms over his chest. "Does the ensemble come with yodeling lessons?"

Neither Aleta, nor the hairstylist, makeup artist, or photographer was amused. The *Seventeen* reporter took notes. Not a good sign.

Jacey looked to Cinnamon to save her. But her agent was striding the room in her slouchy midheel boots, on her cell phone.

The woman who'd arrived with Cinnamon was tall and slim, poured into a black Calvin Klein power suit. Jacey hadn't been introduced, but it had to be her publicist—the one who'd set this up.

"Peyton?" Jacey gave her an imploring look. "I know we haven't met, and I'm beyond grateful you scored me a cover, but—" *I'll be the laughingstock of Hollywood, of Bloomfield Hills High School, of the entire planet!*

Peyton waved her off, put a manicured finger up to her chin, and considered. She addressed only the stylist. "Aleta, you are the best! What an original interpretation of 'wholesome'! We so lucked out getting you as our stylist! Now, we'll shoot Jacey in this scrumptious look, but *of course* we'll do several different looks. I know you want to see her in different palettes. I'm thinking maybe we'll try pinks and blues or go with more muted naturals in some shots. I'm sure you had that planned anyway!"

Aleta beamed.

The sly wink Peyton sent Jacey was clear: *This is how it's done. We don't whine and complain. We manipulate. Watch, listen, and learn.*

Point taken!

Jacey posed against different backdrops, everything from stark white to a sandy beach scene; there was a lush flowering garden, even wallpaper with comedy-tragedy masks. It'd look as if she'd been photographed in various locales.

Best of all, the heinous milkmaid top was soon ditched in favor of some truly kick-ass fashions. She posed in Baby Phat capris, Miss Sixty jeans, Luca Luca miniskirts, various flowy halter tops, Betsey Johnson sundresses, G-Unit tank tops, hand-painted V-neck tops, and a flotilla of footwear, from flip-flops to ankle-strapped shoes to platform slides. Jacey coveted a pair of faded Escada jeans studded with Swarovski crystals.

Her hair was restyled quickly: straightened with bangs; back-curled; done in ringlets, breezy waves, a cute chopstick updo. She wasn't wild about all the styles, but all of them were huge improvements over the Princess Leia–meets Bozo side-tufts.

The thirty-one makeup brushes eventually produced more palatable looks. Jacey was relieved when the makeup artist dialed down the cheeks and lips, and outlined her intense, ocean-colored eyes with kohl.

While she was changing looks and posing, her friends gathered on a slouchy leather couch. Desi was chatting up the *Seventeen* reporter, and paging through copies of the magazines, full of questions. *"Nick's Most Embarrassing Moments,"* she read. "Do you really talk to all the stars, or is some of this stuff made up?"

The reporter, Louise Gordon, was only too happy to dish. She'd been a *Seventeen* correspondent for three years, and had interviewed all the biggies.

Did Ryan really cheat? Were Paris and Nicole ever enemies, or was it just a publicity stunt? Desi was in fan-girl heaven.

"Here's my question," Ivy interrupted. "Are these starlets as stupid as they seem?"

Louise lowered her voice. "If I told you what they were really like, their publicists would never grant me access to another client. So I have to be discreet, y'know?" She shifted her gaze to Peyton.

"Yo, Jace, your cell phone's ringing," Dash called out. "Want me to get it?"

"Would you?"

"Please turn this way, Miss Chandliss, I need a half smile from you," the photographer instructed.

"It's Logan," Dash shouted. "I'll tell him you'll call him back?"

"Tell him I'm in the middle of this photo session . . . and send him kisses."

Dash stuck his finger down his throat at her instructions, causing Jacey's half smile to morph into a full giggle.

"Look at this shot of Nicole!" Desi pointed to a page in the magazine. "Seriously, her head's so big—looks like they planted it on someone else's twig!"

"That's for her ego," Ivy quipped. "It needs a lot of room."

Dash leaned over to see. "They should call these girls *starve*-lets instead of starlets."

Jacey doubled over laughing.

"Miss Chandliss, whenever you're ready to pose for us," the photographer groused, "just let me know."

"Oh, sorry!"

"Now, as we were saying," the photographer continued, "please stand straight, put your hand on your hip, and look over your shoulder. Yes, like that. Good!"

Standing straight was one thing; keeping a straight face was another—her friends were hysterical.

"Oooh, here's next issue's Guys We Love section," Desi gushed.

"Chad! Justin!" Ivy said, joining in. "Look at that shot of Billie Joe! Smokin'!"

Jacey did a double take—really? Preppy Ivy lusting after a punker? Jacey wondered what else about Ivy had changed in college.

"Miss Chandliss, *again*! My time is money. Can you please follow directions and tilt your head to the left, as I asked?"

"What about *him*?" Desi was asking the reporter. "What's he really like?"

"Matt Canseco?" Louise frowned. "Him I know by reputation only—and it is not a pretty one."

Matt Canseco was a daring young Hollywood hipster–slash–movie star—so deliberately out of the mainstream that in some circles he was in.

"So you've never interviewed him?" Dash asked.

"Not for lack of trying," laughed Louise. "Our readers

are fascinated with his whole bad-boy vibe. But Matt would never deign to speak to a teen magazine. He's anti-publicity."

"What's he *into*, then?" Desi piped up.

"Drugs, booze, trashing hotel rooms, slinky Goth girls—that's what I've heard, anyway," Louise said with a shrug.

But he's so talented! Jacey wanted to put her two cents in. She'd seen Matt in arty flicks like *Transgression* and *Soulmates*, plus the recent remake of *The Outsiders* and that R-rated comedy she couldn't remember the title of. Matt was the kind of actor who could play any role and convince you he *was* that character. He was, it suddenly hit her, the kind of actor she wanted to be.

The photographer's young assistant, who'd been checking Dash out, sauntered over to the posse. "That Matt guy? I saw him once at a club. He was trashed, man! I stayed away."

While listening to her friends, an unsettling thought lodged itself in Jacey's brain. Here she was in the harsh glare of the spotlight, the camera clicking away, and they were all there because of her. And she felt invisible. Why?

Maybe because she wasn't having fun. Because no one was asking her opinion or laughing at her bon mot. Her friends were having a blast, dishing about stars, helping themselves to a sugary smorgasbord of tasty treats. Did they even remember she was in the room, posing in a ridiculous outfit in clown makeup and listening to her empty stomach rumble?

Hmmm . . . it struck her that maybe being in the posse was more fun than being the celebrity.

"You're luminous, my girl!" the photographer crowed. "Incandescent!"

Okay, maybe not.

jaceyfan blog

Jacey Disses Paris!?!

Not only did certain members of Jacey's posse totally embarrass themselves and everyone else while they partied just a little too exuberantly at Torrey Pines — it gets worse! Jacey turned down an invite to meet and party with Paris! She hasn't been famous for two minutes and is already too important for an audience with a national icon? Is our sweet Jacey getting a little too big for her be-yoches? And if so, isn't she a little new to be exhibiting bad behavior already? I'm just askin'.

Chapter Three

No, *Really* . . . Shoot Me Now

Toast, in West Hollywood, masqueraded as a corner café, but the showbiz "in" crowd knew it as a chill hangout, understated and hip. Which is why, explained Louise from *Seventeen*, she'd chosen it for their interview.

"They only serve breakfast and lunch, and at this hour, it should be pretty empty, since it's early for the showbiz lunch crowd." It was 3:25 p.m.

The publicist, Peyton, who'd come along, approved.

Jacey liked it immediately. The decor was down-home, upscale, and humorous all at the same time. Large store-front windows set in brick walls kept it sunny, and seating ranged from wooden benches to leather-upholstered booths to couchy love seats. Random life-size papier-mâché sculptures of cows and alligators dotted the restaurant, giving it a funky, kitschy vibe. All it needed was a gift shop to be Cracker Barrel, 90210.

It was the menu, however, that Jacey locked onto. The star was ravenous. She'd been posing, changing, and getting scolded while her friends had been chewing and chatting. She ordered calamari rings and something called Not Your Mom's Grilled Cheese, described as "melted mozzarella and feta cheese, with sun-dried tomatoes, basil, and an olive tapenade on country white bread."

She topped her order off with a large mocha macchiato frappé.

"You're really going to eat all that?" Louise looked scandalized.

"You're really going to write about what I eat?" Jacey returned her look.

The reporter shrugged. "Readers want to know."

"Don't worry—she's going to throw it up as soon as you leave," Dash said in a deadpan voice. Everyone burst out laughing.

Peyton intervened: "I'm sure you realize this is off the record—and they're kidding."

Jacey did the mental translation: *If any of this gets into the article, this'll be the last Jacey Chandliss interview you'll get.* She was liking her publicist more and more.

Her friends ordered quesadillas and burgers. Louise and Peyton stuck with salads. "With the dressing on the side," they chorused to the waiter.

In midmeal, Louise switched on her tape recorder. "We're honored that you've chosen *Seventeen* for your first in-depth interview."

"Uh . . . it's my pleasure." Jacey accidentally dripped melted cheese onto the table.

"Do you read *Seventeen*?" Louise asked, motioning for Jacey to speak into the tape recorder.

"Um, well . . ." Jacey stalled. The real answer was "No."

Peyton jumped in with the interview answer: "As often as she can."

Louise went into standard interviewese, and Jacey coolly handled the softball bio questions lobbed at her.

"When did you first want to be an actress?"

"For as long as I can remember!"

"What was your first role in a play?"

"Toto, in *The Wizard of Oz*, in kindergarten."

"What did you think of the other *Gen Next* contestants?"

"So many amazing talents out there; I wish they could all get this opportunity."

"Do you have a boyfriend?"

"Wanna see a picture?" Jacey grinned and started to open her cell phone, where a photo of Logan—whom she'd called back in the car coming over—was her screen saver.

"Cute guy," said Louise admiringly. "Broad shoulders, blond, blue-eyed . . . so all-American looking!"

"Nice guy," Jacey said. "Smart guy, too—the whole package."

"You know," mused Louise, "the thing I personally find most interesting about you is . . ."—she indicated Ivy, Desi, and Dash—"your friends. Your posse. You guys seem so tight, like you almost have your own secret shorthand. Our readers love friendship stories, especially when they involve celebrities. Is it okay if I ask them a few questions?"

"I don't see why not," Peyton said. Then she whipped out her BlackBerry and attacked her e-mails.

"When did you first meet Jacey?" Louise asked. "What can you tell us that people don't know?"

Ivy went first. "I've known her all her life—I'm her cousin. Our moms are sisters, and we live a few towns away."

"What was she like as a kid?" Louise asked.

"She was . . . very dramatic!" Ivy said with a flourish. "Always acting out TV shows. Like, she'd pretend to be

Elmo from *Sesame Street*, or D.J. on *Full House*. I remember once she spent the day being Angelina Jolie in *Girl, Interrupted*. What a hoot!"

Jacey, groaning, hid behind her hands.

"I notice Jacey's mom isn't here—I guess you're the designated family member and chaperone," Louise said to Ivy.

Ivy conceded that, since she was over twenty-one, and a recent college grad, she'd been available, and psyched, to be Jacey's legal guardian for the summer.

"What about you, Dash? Are you also a relative?"

"He's my soul mate." Jacey spoke for him.

"I'm the boy next door," Dash said with a smile. "We've been friends since first grade."

"We tell each other *everything*," Jacey announced.

Louise eyed Dash coolly. "Mmmm, soul mates, confidants, boy next door. So that'd make you the gay one."

Jacey's hand flew out like a shot. She grabbed the tape recorder and hit STOP. "Why do you need that in the interview?"

Peyton glanced up from her BlackBerry. "What's the matter?"

"That was . . . unnecessary," Jacey said.

Dash shrugged. "No biggie. I've been out for years. I don't care."

Jacey, however, cared a lot. "I don't want that in the interview."

"No problem!" Louise said. "But I'd think you would. Gay best friends are so on trend! And our readers will want to know why Dash isn't your boyfriend."

Peyton calmly took the tape recorder and hit the rewind button before handing it back. "Jacey's right. It's not for *Seventeen* to publish anything private about her friends."

"I didn't mean anything by it, and you have my word, it won't be in the article," Louise, in suck-up mode, assured them.

"Anyone care about me?" Desi finally broke in. "I've actually got a story."

Jacey softened. "Everyone cares about you! Always."

She would never forget the day she had met Desi. It had been one of those truly random encounters that led to two girls from different worlds becoming best friends.

It was at a modeling audition for Hudson's department store. Jacey and her mom were on the escalator going up; Desi and her grandmother were on the parallel down escalator.

Jacey happened to catch sight of the roundest, brownest, friendliest eyes she'd ever seen, and blurted out, "I hope you get chosen!"

"Right back atcha!" Desi responded, not thinking it strange that a girl she didn't know would wish her luck.

Both girls, aged ten at the time, and as different as they could be, ended up among the chosen models for the Girls' Clothes section of the catalog. For Jacey, who'd grown up comfortably in the suburbs, the modeling gig was a frequent after-school activity, when she wasn't doing a play. For Desi, who lived in a trailer with her grandmother, it was nothing short of a miracle.

"Wow," Louise seemed fascinated by Desi's account. "And you're never jealous of her? None of you? It'd be normal if you were—"

Ivy cut her off. "Color us abnormal. She's family."

"Okay, I hear you. One last question, then I'll let you go. Are you aware of the Jaceyfan blog?" Louise asked.

Peyton jumped in, frowning. "You mean the *Generation Next* blog?"

"That's what it used to be. It's now devoted solely to Jacey, written by someone who won't reveal his identity but claims to know everything about her."

"We've seen it," Ivy said tersely.

"We have no comment on that," Peyton added.

"There isn't much to know," Jacey said. "Until *Generation Next*, I was just a girl from Michigan who dreamed of becoming an actress. There aren't any scandals. I'm not secretly dating a rock star old enough to be my dad, starving myself, or betraying my best friend. I don't even have a tattoo! So the blogger has to make things up to make me look bad. It's ridiculous. I'm sure, whoever he is, he'll get tired of me and go bother someone else."

"Otherwise, we reserve our right to litigate," Peyton put in, as if suing people were something she did every day.

"Yeah, the blogger can bring it," Jacey joshed, raising her fist in mock belligerence.

"Great sound bite!" Louise grinned, and she switched off the tape recorder. "I've gotta run—don't want to keep my next interview waiting. I scored Ashlee and Jessica together! Thanks so much for your answers. I know our readers will love it."

"That went well," Peyton said as soon as Louise was out of earshot. "Just one thing, Jacey. It's honorable to stand up for yourself and your friends, but in the future, that's what I'm for. Publicists play the bad guy."

"You give good bad guy, Peyton. Thank you."

Peyton's smile was warm and genuine. "That's what I'm here for. But I gotta run—is it safe if I take care of the bill and leave you guys alone here? You're not gonna trash the place, or get kicked out or anything?"

As soon as she left, Jacey heaved a sigh of relief. "Alone at last! Gawd, I thought they'd never leave!"

"Me, too!" said Ivy, standing up. "I've had to hit the ladies' room for, like, the last half hour, but I didn't want to miss anything! Be right back."

"Do you think the *Seventeen* babe is really gonna write all that?" Desi wondered aloud.

"What I think," Dash decided, "is that our little Peyton earns her paycheck by making sure the article is gushing, complimentary, and devoid of all controversy. I wonder how much money she makes."

"Whatever she makes, she's worth it," said Jacey. "Don't you agree?"

A few minutes later, Ivy returned from the ladies' room, looking worried. "We got a problem."

Ivy pointed outside, where several dozen paparazzi— men with huge cameras hanging around their necks—had materialized. They looked like predators, waiting to pounce on unsuspecting prey.

"Who's here?" Jacey sat upright and looked around. "Lindsay? Mary-Kate?"

"No, duh-head, you are!" Desi jumped up to get a better look.

"Me?" Jacey scoffed. "No way. My movie didn't even come out yet. I'm not famous enough for paparazzi."

"Excuse me, winner of *Generation Next*? You were on TV every week for months. Trust me, you're famous enough." Dash was obviously concerned about the crowd outside the café.

"Should I call Peyton?" Desi asked. "Maybe she's still around."

"No, don't do that," Jacey said. "If you're right, and they're here because they want a picture of me, so what? Did I not just subject myself to five grueling hours of posing for pictures? What's a few more? We'll just walk out, I'll pose, and we'll get in the car and go. We can do this."

"We need a plan," Dash insisted. "How about Des and I walk on either side of you while Ivy goes ahead and gets the car?"

"Or, does like Lassie," Desi quipped, "and goes for help!"

They would need it.

No sooner had the foursome exited the restaurant than chaos erupted—the photographers rushed Jacey, crushing and elbowing each other out of the way, snapping flashes in Jacey's eyes, vying for her attention, barraging her with questions.

Her friends got separated instantly, rudely pushed and shoved away from Jacey. A swarm of shutterbugs closed in on her, clicking away, calling out, "Jacey! Look this way!"

"Hey starlet—over here!" "Who's that guy you had lunch with? Your boyfriend?" "Are the rumors true about you dissing Paris?"

The fight-or-flight instinct kicked in: Jacey chose flight. She backed up, trying to create some personal space, imploring them to "Wait! Stop! Hang on a minute!"

No one paid attention. She had at least a dozen lenses shoved in her face. If only she could have reached out and swatted them all away! Panic rose. She choked it down.

Okay, I can do this, she told herself. If they just give me one tiny speck of air, one millisecond.

The only way to get it was to hold up her hand and cover her face—a picture not many of the photographers seemed to want. It gave Jacey just enough time to compose herself, take a deep breath, and smile brightly.

She hoped to appease them, so they'd get what they'd come for—and go home. She turned this way and that, so each could get a head-on shot. She even waved.

That worked! For a second. Then one of the cameramen tripped over another, causing a domino effect. Unsurprisingly, a blame-o-rama broke out. Fists and curses flew; cameras swung out.

One voice rang out above the commotion: "Jacey, duck!" It was Dash.

A camera had been knocked out of someone's hand,

and it flew through the air, nearly clipping her head. Okay, panic was the appropriate response now!

Jacey attempted to retreat into the restaurant, but the entrance was choked with lensmen. She executed a soccer move—faking to the right, then fleeing to the left, but her pathetic attempts at escape brought the fighting photographers' attention right back to her.

Where were the police? Why hadn't someone from Toast come out to break this up? Where were her friends? How was she going to get out of this?

It took the screeching of tires, the acrid stench of burnt rubber, and a blaring car horn to bring the chaos to a momentary halt.

Yess! The cops *had* arrived!

Or . . . had they? The car coming to her rescue was a screaming red Dodge Viper convertible. Jacey was fairly sure that even in Hollywood, cops didn't drive hot sports cars with sticker prices starting at $85,000. The snazzy two-seater nosed its way right into the throng and up onto the sidewalk, forcing the paparazzi to scatter like marbles. The passenger-side door swung open, and a cute young guy leaned out, shouting, "Jump in the back!"

Jacey froze. The cameras started clicking, the paparazzi charging toward her once again like a herd of crazed buffalo. She heard Desi wail, "Jace, wait! I'm here," and "Let me get through! Outta the way!"

"Come on, both of you, we'll get you out of here," beckoned the guy holding the car door open. "Hurry up!" He pulled his seat forward to make room for them.

Jacey's heart hammered. Miraculously, Desi made it to her side at that moment. The girls wedged themselves into the tiny, not-meant-for-humans rear compartment of the car. The door slammed. Instantly, the driver shifted into reverse and backed out, not bothering to check whether anyone was in the way.

Saved! Whew!

By . . . whom? It'd happened so fast—*was happening* so fast—they didn't even know who they were getting into a car with. What if these two were kidnappers and she'd just jumped from being paparazzi bait to being the subject of a ransom note? Jacey tried to see their faces, but the car was racing down the street, her hair was flying in her face, and she could barely move, stuck on her knees in the tiny space behind the driver's seat, squished next to Desi.

The driver was careening down the street like a maniac, seemingly taking corners on two wheels? Desi was trying to say something to Jacey, but with the wind swirling around her head, she couldn't hear. Okay, she told herself, this wasn't gonna be her day to die under a herd of mad photographers—she'd be killed in a fiery crash instead!

Finally, when they'd gotten far from the paparazzi, the driver slowed down enough for Jacey to catch the scent of Ivory soap and fresh, woodsy aftershave, to brush the hair out of her eyes, and notice the driver's dark shades and a navy blue baseball cap set low over his brow. Not a good sign—her rescuer-slash-madman obviously didn't want to be recognized. She gulped.

She focused on the guy riding shotgun, the dude who'd lured them into the car. He also wore a baseball cap—his was on backward with a . . . yellow Tweety Bird logo?

She relaxed slightly. Seriously, what self-respecting celebri-napper would wear a Tweety Bird cap?

They could, of course, have been garden-variety lunatics. *"I tawt I taw a lu-na-tic,"* Jacey recited, and she burst out laughing. Oh, God, she was losing it!

Blessedly, the next traffic light was red. Even better, the car stopped. Tweety swung around, and Jacey and Desi got a first good look at him.

Jacey's first impression was of a wholesome frat boy. Not brandishing a weapon; that was good. Unless you counted his killer blue eyes. They could render a girl helpless.

"Are you ladies okay?" he asked.

Desi, white-knuckled, still breathing hard from the scuffle earlier, nodded.

Probably, their rescuers were just a couple of slacker scions, playing hero for a day. Jacey calmed herself with that new description.

Then the driver turned around. Off came the cap, followed by the sunglasses.

These were not cops, kidnappers, lunatics, or slacker-boys.

Jacey had been rescued by a movie star. And his exceptionally hot friend.

Jacey Flees Photogs!

Is America's sweetheart suddenly too good for us? Exiting a trendy restaurant, Jacey was met by a group of photographers just wanting a photo of her. Instead of posing, grateful for their interest, she flipped out! Acted like she'd been attacked by a swarm of killer bees! Jacey, sweetheart, get a clue: your movie hasn't even come out yet. This "I'm Too Good to Pose" attitude? Bad sign! Bad It girl! Unless you felt . . . bloated. Do you even know how many calories were in that grilled cheese you hoovered?

Chapter Four

Dungeons and Dragonesses

"Matt Canseco! Oh, my God!" Desi was hyperventilating. Being catapulted from one terrifyingly surreal "only in Hollywood" scenario right into another had literally taken her breath away. She reached for her inhaler—something she hadn't needed in months.

"Oh, my God! Oh, my God! Are you really . . . *you*?" Desi managed to get out between breaths.

Good-natured chuckling came from the front seat as Matt checked the side-view mirror. "I seem to be me, yeah. Are you okay? You need a doctor or something?"

"You *saved* us! Oh, my God, we got saved by Matt Canseco!" The only thing that stopped Desi from reaching for her cell phone was the inability to breathe.

"Sure you're all right?" Matt asked again. "Cedars-Sinai hospital isn't far from here."

Jacey gripped the back of Matt's headrest and leaned forward. "Give her a minute to calm down. She'll be okay. But, look, thank you so much! That was . . . I didn't expect to be mobbed like that. . . . I thought I was going to be trampled to death."

"Hey, you're welcome. Me and my buddy Rob were on our way to grab a bite and saw that insane scene going down."

Tweety turned and extended his hand. "Hi, I'm Rob O'Shay."

Desi shook his hand. "I'm Desiree Paczki and this is . . ."

"Jacey," Matt said. "Yeah, we heard the shouting."

Jacey's cell phone rang and she managed to grab it just before it went into voice mail. "It's Ivy," she told Desi. "We're fine, thanks. We got kinda rescued. We'll be home in a few. We're fine. Promise."

"Jacey," Rob mused, trying to place her. "You're from that reality show. Was it the beach show with the bitchy girls in bikinis? Or the singing one with the bitchy judge?"

Matt punched his buddy lightly in the arm. "She's the actress. The one who got the part in *Four Sisters*."

"*Four Sisters*?" Rob repeated, searching his memory.

"Why does that sound familiar?"

"Gina Valentine. That's why. Your . . . *ahem* . . . *friend* auditioned for the role of the youngest sister," Matt reminded him. He checked Jacey in the rearview mirror. His lips curved upward. "That's the part you got, right?"

"That's the one." Jacey was puzzled. "I don't understand how your friend auditioned for it." There was no one named Gina on *Generation Next*.

"More than auditioned," Matt said. "She was told she got the part of Ava."

"Yeah," Rob agreed with a rueful laugh. "She nailed it. They told her agent that she had it. *Then* the producers made a deal with the *Generation Next* people—that role would go to the winner of the TV show. Snap! Gina didn't have the role anymore."

Jacey didn't know what to say. Was there a diplomatic response to this?

"I'm out here to do some publicity, and for the premiere," she offered. "I'm sorry about your friend."

"So, where are we taking you ladies?" Rob changed the subject. "And can you manage back there?"

Jacey began to give Matt directions, but as soon as she said "Burbank" he knew.

"The Oakwood Apartments on Barham Boulevard, right? Everyone who comes out here bunks there, until they buy a house or something."

"I'm just here for the summer, won't be buying a house," Jacey said.

"You should stay," said Matt. "If you want to be an actor, that is. Los Angeles is where you have to be—whether you like it or not."

"You don't?" Desi asked.

"Matt and I are more New York than L.A.," Rob explained. "What about you?"

When Desi said the name of her hometown, Matt practically slammed on the brakes. "Hamtramck? Really? Oh, man, I haven't thought about that place in years! You from there?"

Desi was taken aback. Who had ever heard of Hamtramck? "It's a small neighborhood on the outskirts of—"

"Detroit, yeah, sure, I know. My grandpops worked at the GM plant here. Spent every summer with him when I was a kid. To this day, I only drive American cars!"

Matt and Desi got into a spirited game of Hamtramck geography, comparing hangouts, pizza places, even Kowalski's Deli. It was possible, they decided, that Matt's gramps and Desi's grandmother might even know each other!

"If not, maybe we could introduce them," Desi chuckled.

Matt cracked up. "Yeah, an old-people hookup. That'd be fun."

They turned into the Oakwood Apartments complex, and Jacey directed Matt to their building.

"Thank you guys so much! Do you want to come in for a drink or something?" Jacey asked.

"We gotta book," Rob replied. "Maybe another time."

Matt took his sunglasses off again and stared at her. And Jacey found herself staring back, into the deepest bittersweet-chocolate eyes she'd ever seen, ringed by eyelashes so long and dark they should be illegal on guys.

Matt seemed amused. "So, later, me and the guys'll probably hang out at Dungeon, if you want to come."

"It's a small bar in Eagle Rock," Rob said. "We usually get there around eleven. It's low-key."

"Yeah!" Desi lit up. "We haven't been anywhere fun— well, except for the spa, and we had to leave early—and we've been here almost two full weeks!"

"Wait, hang on," Jacey said. "I have an early meeting tomorrow with my agent, and . . ." She trailed off, annoyed with herself. The newbie telling a movie star *she* had a meeting with her agent. Lame!

Matt winked. "We'll getcha home by, what, maybe four or five in the morning. You'll have plenty of time to make your meeting."

Rob opened the car door, and Desi jumped out. "Give us the address. We'll be there."

Matt seemed to be waiting for an answer—as if he were serious about the invitation. How ridiculous did Jacey feel, on her knees, in a no-backseat sports car? Her mouth opened, and to her horror, stupid things dribbled out.

"I have other friends here."

Matt chewed on a toothpick. "Bring 'em."

Jacey noticed his license plate as he drove away: INDISPRT.

Dungeon was a dusky, dank dive bar. A place so under the radar that no one even needed a fake ID to get in. The purple ceiling lamps illuminated the haze of smoke that hung in the air, and not much else. Obsessing over what to wear had been unnecessary, Jacey realized, blinking as her eyes adjusted. The cavernous chamber was so dark she doubted anyone would be able to appreciate her hip-hugging, low-rise jeans; chocolate-and-cocoa-colored, beaded, scoop-neck top; and leather peace-symbol choker.

Not that anyone was there yet.

No one who mattered, anyway. Dungeon was littered with random clusters of, "tattooed, pierced, Mohawk-sporting, fishnet-wearing rabble," as Dash drolly observed.

Matt Canseco was not there. Nor was Rob O'Shay, nor

anyone who looked remotely semi–demi–quasi-famous.

Jacey, Desi, Dash, and Ivy had arrived around eleven fifteen, planning to be casually late. Instead, they were either hopelessly early or in the wrong dungeon—that, or they'd been Punk'd.

"Are you sure this is the right place?" Ivy asked doubtfully, clutching the Dior Gaucho saddle tote—a gift from Jacey—close to her body.

"Did it ever occur to you," Dash asked, "that Matt Canseco was putting you on? How funny would it be to send the newbie and her sheltered, suburban friends to a hard-core punk shack?"

"Me not sheltered. Me not suburban," Desi grunted playfully.

"The magazine writer said Matt has a nasty rep," Ivy pointed out. "This could be his idea of a joke."

"The *Seventeen* writer never met him," Jacey reminded Ivy. "He wasn't being a jerk when he saved our butts."

"No disrespect, Your Heinie-ness," Dash teased, "but just because someone saves your life doesn't mean they want to hang out with you."

Ivy sighed and looked around. She pointed to a table in the middle of the room. "We're here already. We'll give them a half hour and leave if they don't show. Anyway, I wouldn't mind a drink."

"I'd love a frothy strawberry daiquiri," Jacey said, her mouth watering.

"I'm going straight to tequila," Dash decided, "if we can find a waiter to take our order."

Desi licked her lips. "I wouldn't mind a snack. Let's get a menu."

Fifteen minutes went by. Neither waiter nor menu materialized.

"I wonder what other stars will show up." Desi scanned the cavernous room.

"Forget Paris or Lindsay," Dash deadpanned. "No mirrors."

"Twenty minutes," Ivy reported, checking her watch. "Ten more, then we leave."

"Without even one measly drink?" Desi whined. "I'm going to the bar."

Jacey arched her back and craned her neck to have a better look around. No luck. Just uncool club kids and Goth girls, clustered around small tables, smoking, drinking, and swaying to the music.

Suddenly, a familiar scent wafted by: an intoxicating mix of woodsy aftershave, weathered leather, and soap. It was getting stronger. It was right over her shoulder.

"So, how come no one's drinking at this table?" Matt Canseco teased. "Unless you're waiting for service. If you are, you came to the wrong place!"

Jacey whirled around and caught her breath.

Even without good lighting, Matt looked amazing in a worn brown Belstaff leather bomber jacket over a black T-shirt that said 1-800-AUTOPSY. She stuttered, "I didn't see you come in."

"Not through the front door, no."

Desi was impressed. "A back door! Very cool."

"There are ways . . ." Matt shook a finger at them mock-reproachfully, "to elude the paparazzi—not that they'd come here. Neighborhood's too out of the way, and too dangerous."

Dash's eyes widened.

"My buddies are over there." Matt nodded in the direction of the bar, where three guys, one of whom was a Tweety-less Rob, were huddled, ordering drinks.

They all trooped up to the bar.

Rob gave Desi and Jacey hugs. His dark, slick hair stood up in porcupine spikes. Contrasted with his blue eyes and freshly scrubbed baby face, it was a kind of jarring look—rock star meets the Sprouse twins.

The short, muscular dude with long blond hair grazing his shoulder, wearing a white T-shirt, was Emilio. A lean, lanky guy with a diamond nostril-stud introduced himself as Aja.

"Asia? Like the continent?" Ivy asked, intrigued.

"Like the Steely Dan album," he replied with a grin. "My parents were big classic rock fans." He eyed Dash. "Guessing yours were mystery buffs?"

Dash was impressed. "My father is an English professor at University of Michigan. I was named for Dashiell Hammett, the writer. Didn't think anyone out here would make that connection."

"Not out there they won't. In here, you got a shot," Matt snorted.

"Dungeon's a hangout for arty types," Emilio explained, motioning around the room. "Starving artists, musicians, poets, actors, screenwriters, people hoping to make a living at their art."

"All except Matt," Rob teased. "Bro's here to hang on to his rapidly fading street cred."

Matt jokingly punched him. "I'm here 'cause I can't take you guys anywhere else."

The bartender, Tina, blended with the scenery. She had short black hair with glow-in-the-dark orange streaks, an eyebrow ring, thick eyeliner, and tarantula eyelashes. A tricep tattoo read, DESTINY. "'Sup, Matt," she greeted him. "You having the usual?"

The usual turned out to be beer, which turned out to be the drink of choice for everyone except Aja, who had a vodka stinger, and Dash, who suddenly decided that that was what he wanted, too.

Jacey had been craving something pink and frothy— only . . . she checked her environment again. Probably not available in a dive bar. Ivy ordered a bottle of red wine to share with her.

The group migrated to the far corner of the room, where they pushed two small tables together and crowded around. Ivy had asked Matt to order some appetizers. "Everything's on us," she told him. "It's our way of saying thanks for what you did today."

"If I'd known you were treating," Matt said, pouring the wine for Ivy and Jacey, "I would've suggested some place with sushi, caviar, and flavored martinis. We'll have to make do with potato skins, calamari, and guacamole."

"Here's to Matt and Rob, who swooped in and saved my butt today." Jacey raised her wineglass.

"And a lovely *tuchis* it is!" Emilio cracked, raising his beer stein. "Hear, hear!"

"So, tell us all about the rescue mission." Aja dipped a chip into the guacamole as soon as it hit the table. "All Matt said was that he and Rob picked up a couple of cuties on the street."

"Street cuties," put in Emilio, who'd obviously started his own private party before arriving at Dungeon. "That could be the next big reality show—*America's Next Top Street Hos!*

"Not going there, Emilio," Jacey said, suddenly realizing how strange this was. She hadn't even known these people twelve hours ago, and now they were kidding around with one another like old friends. Was there something about Hollywood that made people fast friends?

"How'd the paparazzi even know where I'd be?" she asked.

Matt nursed his beer. "Someone tipped them off. Paparazzi and the tabloids pay for celebrity sightings. Anyone with info who wants to make a buck makes a phone call."

"So, it could have been anyone at the photo session," Jacey said.

Aja shrugged. "Dude, anyone in the restaurant who recognized her—and look, she's there being interviewed, so she's gotta be *someone*."

"Is it really that big a deal?" Emilio asked Jacey. "They were just taking your picture."

"They practically trampled me!" Jacey shivered at the memory of how terrified she'd been when they had all come at her like that, in a pack.

"If you haven't been the target," Matt said, validating her feelings, "you can't imagine how freakin' scary it can be—especially for her. She's like a newborn in the woods o' Holly."

"Have you been a victim of paparazzi hunts, too?" Desi asked.

"After my first movie, but not lately," Matt answered. "I stick with small films, little indies. And out-of-the-way places."

"What's your next movie?" Jacey asked.

"Looks like I'll be doing *Dirt Nap*."

"*Dirt Nap*?" Desi giggled. "Sounds like a movie about street-kid kindergartners."

Matt laughed. "Not close. It's directed by this amazing guy, Noel Langer. No one's ever heard of him, but I'm betting he'll be the next Clint Eastwood, or James Cameron, even."

"See that guy over there?" Rob pointed to a gangly guy with thinning hair and thick, black-framed glasses. He was crouched near a small table in the opposite corner of the bar, talking to a woman. "That's him."

"He's a struggling director," Emilio put in. "Hence, he hangs here, where everything's cheap!"

The music had suddenly gotten louder and changed to a hip-hop mix, and several people got up on the makeshift dance floor.

Ivy went to the bar and returned with another bottle

of wine, jovially offering drinks all around. Emilio guzzled his second or third beer. He turned to Ivy. "So, if you're Jacey's cousin, you're representing for the family, huh?"

The DJ had just put on the Black Eyed Peas. Ivy responded by kicking off her shoes and shouting, "Oh, my God, I love this song! I'm *so* dancing—who's coming with me?"

Emilio didn't need any further invitation. Surfer Boy was on Ivy's heels. He was half a head shorter than Jacey's lanky cousin, but soon they were bumping and grinding as Ivy, well on her way to being sloshed, shouted out the lyrics: *"My lovely lady bumps!"* Clearly, Emilio agreed with that assessment.

Jacey leaned in toward Matt. "Do you think they'll print those pictures? I look really stupid, like I'm running for my life."

Matt shrugged. "Who cares? You weren't trashed . . . or naked. I mean, if someone took a picture here, that'd be a reason to worry."

Just then, the Black Eyed Peas smoothly gave way to Shakira. Matt grabbed Desi's hand. "Hamtramck! Let's get on the dance floor and show 'em how they do this in the Motor City!"

Jacey's petite pal was all over that! She got up, shaking her ample tail feathers as she hit the dance floor.

Matt's arms flew into the air; he was snapping his fingers, and his hips were . . . swiveling?

Jacey threw her head back and laughed. If the paparazzi could have seen him now! He was living proof that white guys, in fact, couldn't dance—no matter what 'hood they said they were from! Matt "Too Cool for the Room" Canseco looked as dorky as a geek on prom night, having a complete blast.

Jacey jumped up, practically wrenched Rob out of his seat, and sashayed onto the dance floor, taking a spot next to Matt, Desi, Ivy, and Emilio. She knew how to dance. Watch me now, her body language said, as she writhed and gyrated, woozily losing herself in the music. Soon she was sweating, her top clinging to her body. It was a good sweat. The kind that comes from dirty-dancing with— hello!—a sexy movie star and his friends, your very first time in a club in L.A. Does it get any better than that?

She felt a tap on her shoulder. "Look who's here, in *my* place, dancing with *my* friends. It's Scene-stealer Barbie!" a girl in a spray-painted-on mini and furry jacket snarled.

"Oh, look! It's a Bratz doll—and all her slutty parts move," Ivy shot back, without missing a beat.

"Who're you? Willow, the bean-stalk bodyguard?" the angry girl snapped, as she circled around Ivy.

"A bean stalk with better taste than you," Ivy retorted,

giving her no quarter. "How many Muppets died making that jacket?"

Matt inserted himself between the warring factions. "Whoa, whoa, chill—what's going on, anyway?" He put an arm around the girl, who had topped off her mini with a plunging V-neck top under the fuzzy open jacket. "Easy there, Gina. Play nice."

Gina ignored him, moving closer to Ivy, death rays shooting from her eyes.

Jacey's stomach muscles clenched. Gina Valentine. In the house, in their faces. Insane over losing the part in *Four Sisters*—to her.

Gina inched forward slowly.

Ivy clamped a hand on Jacey's shoulder, pushing her away, and snapped at the intruder.

"I don't know who you are, but you're rude and crude. No one talks to my girl like that." Ivy, who could not have passed a sobriety test at that moment, came off as serious as a heart attack.

And that was pretty much all the provocation the rude, crude intruder needed. Gina, who looked as if she had cut her own hair with a butter knife, was brimming with fire and sass. Her face darkened, and not only because her eye makeup was smeared. "Your girl, huh? Don't you mean the starlet, Hollywood's new It girl—

whether she deserves it or not?"

Officially scared now, Jacey was ready for someone to break the fight up. But everyone—Dash, Rob, Emilio, Aja, even Matt—seemed paralyzed, unsure what was about to happen. Would this blow up into a full-on fight scene or fade to a commercial? Should she, maybe, apologize to Gina . . . or something?

Desi made the decision for them. All of four feet eleven inches on a good day, Desiree was locked, loaded, and up in Gina's face in no time, snarling, "Who exactly do you think you are, busting in and dissing my friend?"

"I'm the actress she stepped all over, that's who."

"She didn't step on anybody!" Desi growled. "Apologize. Now."

Gina stuck her chin out defiantly. "Make me, half-pint."

"Bring it on, bee-yotch!" Desi balled up her fists. Ivy was right behind her.

The crowd, previously borderline comatose, came alive. "Chick fight over here! Smack-down over there!"

It happened fast. Gina lurched forward, grabbed a handful of Desi's curls, and pulled hard. Desi shook her off, laughing. "That's how you fight here? Shee-it." She swung an uppercut and connected with Gina's jaw, hooting, "There—now you can play a patient on *Grey's*

Anatomy, and you won't need makeup!"

Enraged, Gina came back, eyes ablaze. "You don't know who you're messing with." Her fist flew out, but Desi ducked.

Gina's posse moved in. One of them jabbed Desi in the belly, and the other connected with a right hook to a spot near Desi's eye, which seemed to be the cue the guys were waiting for. All of them suddenly scrambled to pull the girls apart. Matt, Emilio, and Rob pulled Gina and her scruffy friends off Desi. At the same time, Jacey and Dash sprang into action, pulling Desi toward the door.

Ivy tossed $200 on the table and called out, "It's been real! Keep the change."

Jacey Chick Fight
Breaks Out in Dive Bar!

Jacey and her posse had a night to remember, all right—or maybe a nightmare best forgotten! Where to begin? Let's see, last time I checked, the legal drinking age in this state was twenty-one. So that means, *no way* could that've been Jacey "America's Sweetheart" Chandliss guzzling wine in a public place!

Waaay!

Sorry to sully her image. Not! But that's just what she was doing, getting smashed, dirty-dancing, and—wait, here's the biggie—getting so rowdy she got into a chick fight with actress wannabe and reputed troublemaker Gina Valentine!

So how'd our sweet, wholesome Jace end up with her face in a place like that? Might wanna ask Matt "Bad Boy" Canseco, Jacey's new BFF.

Chapter Five

"But What's My Motivation?" She Whined

It was ten the next morning when a sleep-deprived Jacey and her friends dragged themselves into a glass-and-chrome high-rise building in Beverly Hills and took the elevator to Cinnamon Jones's ninth-floor office.

Jacey's power agent, barely visible behind the piled-high mess on her desk (a mixed-up stack of scripts, paper coffee cups, yellow legal pads, and photos), was multi-tasking, smoothly segueing from phone to computer screen to BlackBerry. Without taking her eyes off the computer monitor she snapped, "You're hungover. All of you."

"Your point . . . ?" Desi demanded, crossing her arms defensively.

"Sulky, too." Cinnamon swiveled around in her leather

chair so that she was facing them. She leveled her gaze at Desi. "I assume the other person looks worse?"

Desi grinned. "Much . . . Ouch! Sorry, it hurts to smile."

Cinnamon punched in four digits on the phone. "Not a problem. There are several items on our agenda that won't make you smile."

"What's wrong?" Dash asked nervously.

Cinnamon shot him a look.

"I mean, besides . . . the . . . uh . . . stuff we know about," he added.

Cinnamon's assistant, Kia, came on the speakerphone. "Do you need me?"

"I need an ice pack in here. We have an injury. Thanks."

"If you mean the blog," Desi piped up, "they can't prove Jacey was drinking."

"Doesn't matter," Cinnamon said. "It's out there. People will believe it."

"Ivy paid in cash," Dash put in. "There's no paper trail of Jacey buying anything."

"Good thinking," Cinnamon conceded. "Let's start with happy news."

"Good, 'cause I'm beyond my quota of crap news," Jacey quipped as she, Ivy, Desi, and Dash planted themselves on the long, low-slung sofa across from

Cinnamon's desk. Ivy took out a notepad, and Dash used his Sidekick—a gift from Jacey. Desi pressed the ice pack to her face, while Jacey sat back and crossed her legs.

Cinnamon favored them with her first genuine grin of the day. "Actually, it's *fabulous* news! What I'm hearing is that you are phenomenal in *Four Sisters*. You steal the movie from Sierra, Kate, and Julia."

Jacey cringed. She was officially a repeat offender. She had stolen the role *and* the picture. Yeah, she could see her popularity soaring in Hollywood.

"That's so awesome, Jacey!" Desi knocked knuckles with her.

"Who's saying that?" Ivy asked cautiously.

"The trades, the gossips, the Web, the insider networks," the agent said, brushing off the question. "Doesn't matter. What matters is they think you're hot—they smell money—and I'm getting calls, offers, bribes . . ." She paused for effect. ". . . And some heavy-duty scripts, with top talent attached."

"But no one's seen *Four Sisters*. How do they know anything?" Jacey asked in a small voice.

Cinnamon chortled. Little crow's-feet around her eyes crinkled. "Lesson one. In this town, it's all about perception. No one 'knows' anything; everyone pretends they do. If they think you're hot, consider yourself scorching!"

Dash asked, "How many offers has she actually gotten?"

"Between people who've called, written, sent flowers, Coach bags, and Judith Ripka jewelry? Let's see. Dozens. Everything from cable TV . . . feh! . . . to network, plus miniseries and features. Which means she's not typecast yet. It's a *fabulous* position to be in."

Jacey's tummy twisted; it was a borderline panic alert. She felt good about her performance in the movie, but seriously, she wasn't eighteen yet. What did she know? The movie could be edited to make her look bad, or . . . maybe she really wasn't that great, and people would find out when the movie came out. Expectations were high.

"This is a good thing!" Cinnamon reassured them.

"So, how does this work?" Dash asked, pointing to the stacks on Cinn's desk. "If there are dozens of scripts there, could we divide them up, each read a bunch?"

"No, no, no! We have *people* for that! We've pared the choices down to four."

"Using what criteria?" Dash wanted to know. "I mean, who decided which are the best four?"

Ruh-roh. Dash had just insulted Cinn's expertise. Bad dog.

Luckily, Cinnamon didn't insult easily. "This is what I

do. This is what I get paid the big bucks for. I guide careers. And I'm damn good at it. So, listen—and learn."

Cinnamon explained, without condescending, that the road to stardom, and the freedom and megabucks that went with it, was tricky. If Jacey were to have her choice of good roles, she had to demonstrate her agility in different genres. "*Four Sisters* is a weepy family drama; hence, your next movie—and it should absolutely be a feature film—don't even think about TV—should be a comedy, an action flick, a romance, a mystery, even a horror flick, as long as it's well done and it's PG or PG-13. No R-rated movies for you yet."

"So," Dash said, "you whittled the offers down to those kinds of films?"

Cinn nodded. "You're learning. But I also ditched anything where the entire movie would rest on Jacey's shoulders alone. There are a zillion reasons why movies fail—I never want Jacey in the position of being blamed."

"I agree!" Jacey blurted out.

Desi wanted to know: "Is there a teen movie? Like a sequel to *How to Lose a Guy in 10 Days*, or *The Princess Diaries*? Jacey would rock that!"

"That's for people just starting out. She's already beyond that, thanks to *Four Sisters*." Cinnamon waved the question away. "I junked those."

"What about indies? I heard about something called *Dirt Nap.*" Jacey was curious about Matt's next film.

"You don't do indies." Cinnamon looked miffed. "You don't need to. Indies are for when you have a string of failures, and you need cred to resurrect your career. Besides, it's not your image."

Dash elbowed her. "America's sweetheart, right?"

"Do you have a problem with that?" Cinnamon was becoming annoyed. "Do you have any idea how many girls out there would give anything to be in her designer sneakers?"

Gina Valentine, for one, Jacey thought guiltily, as she uncrossed her legs and tucked her hundred-dollar Gwen Stefani–designed gold L.A.M.B. sneakers under the couch.

"We can grow you in any direction, at our own pace." Cinnamon was warming to her topic. "You've got time to do the Gwynnie Paltrow classics. Time for small, quirky pieces like the Maggie Gyllenhaals, the Claire Daneses do. In a few years, we'll bring out your sexy side. We are truly going about building a career, a brand."

"A brand?" Ivy was perplexed. "Like Pepsi? Or Cheerios . . ."

"Exactly," Cinnamon said with ease. "Jacey will be as recognizable as Jessica Simpson. There can be a Jacey perfume, a J-Cool clothing line. Anyway, that's for our next meeting. I've put an image consultant on staff. We'll see what he thinks."

"And now . . ." Cinnamon segued to her next topic. "About yesterday. That debacle with the paparazzi. Listen closely: it cannot happen again."

Over the protests of "It wasn't my fault!" and "We couldn't help it!" and "They charged at us!" Cinnamon calmly said, "Peyton will now stay with you during and after all interviews. In addition, I've hired a media adviser—for all of you. Handling paparazzi is an art, and you need to learn it. We can't have any more of this"—she held up copies of the *Star*, the *Enquirer*, *In Touch*, and *OK!* magazine—"ever."

The full-page photos, when taken together, formed a filmstrip of Jacey hiding her face, running away, panicking, appearing as if she really were trying to skip out of her sworn celeb-duty to pose.

"That is so unfair!" Jacey jumped to her feet. "They were gonna run me down!"

Cinn sighed audibly. "Doesn't matter. What they print is what the public believes. Don't sweat that—it gets worse. Riding off with Matt Canseco? Do you have any idea what his image is?"

"He saved us!" Desi shouted.

Cinnamon ignored her. "And going to that dive bar last

night? What were you thinking? Not the kind of place you should be seen at."

"There weren't any photographers there," Ivy reminded her.

"And yet, Mr. Jaceyfan Blogger knew exactly where you were," Cinnamon shot back. "And about that—who is this guy? Where's he getting his info?"

"Can't you hire someone to find out?" Dash asked. "You just hired an image consultant, a media adviser, and a publicist. Isn't there, like, a private detective or something you could hire?"

Cinnamon was not amused.

And neither was Jacey. Hours later, her mood had still not improved. Sure, she was pumped about the *fabulous* buzz for *Four Sisters*, but pretty much everything else about the meeting with Cinnamon annoyed her. "Who is she to tell me I can't hang out with Matt Canseco? She's not my mother!"

"She didn't say you couldn't hang out with him," Dash reminded her. "She said, don't be *seen* with Matt, that's all."

"So you're defending her?" Jacey challenged.

"She's doing her job," Dash said wearily.

"And what's up with J-clothing? And Stinky-J perfume? Whoever said I wanted to be a brand?"

"She's throwing out ideas," Ivy said. "Not orders.

Relax."

"I don't want to relax. I don't need an image *or* a consultant to show me how to keep one. And I don't need a media adviser—I can handle reporters and photographers, as long as they're not coming at me like a pack of vicious velociraptors! This isn't fun."

"Neither is the fact that you're taking your bad mood out on us," Ivy said. "I think Desi and I need a little retail therapy—and you, cranky little cousin, need a nap."

Dash raised his hand. "I volunteer to babysit Jacey."

Jacey was ready to clobber him.

"And," he added, pretending to fend her off, "read the scripts Cinnamon gave us."

"Come on, Dash," Jacey whined after Ivy and Desi had left the apartment. "You know what I'm freaking out about. What happened to just being an actress?"

Dash draped a reassuring arm around her. "Maybe there is no such thing as 'just an actress.' Maybe if you hadn't gotten so famous so fast, or stuck with high school plays . . ." He trailed off, having made his point.

Then he made another: "About Matt Canseco? Please don't tell me you're into him."

Jacey turned on Dash so fast his head spun. "What's up with you and Aja? There was a total connection last night. Do. Not. Deny. It!"

Dash flushed. "We traded phone numbers—don't change the subject. I say this as your friend, Jacey. A few hours in a club with Matt doesn't mean he's into you."

"Who said he was?" she asked. "And if he is? Is that a bad thing?"

"If you get hurt it is."

Jacey brushed him off. "Come on, Dash. I have a boyfriend. I'm crazy about my boyfriend—and I'm loyal to my boyfriend. Matt Canseco is a hot movie star. Who wouldn't want to hang out with him? I don't appreciate my agent telling me I can't. That's what I'm pissed about."

Dash folded his arms. "Yeah, right. Like I can't read you."

"Right now you can't."

"Listen, Jacey, if Matt is into anyone—and I'm not saying he is—the 'connection,' as you put it, is with Desi. Not you."

"Desi?" She arched her eyebrows. "I don't think so."

"You don't think so? Or you don't want to think so—or you don't think she's worthy of him."

"Dashiell Walker! How could you say that?"

"Only to make sure you're not thinking that. And if you are, to point out how truly obnoxious and wrongheaded that would be."

Jacey narrowed her eyes. She was not happy with

Dash just then. "Don't lecture me, Dash. Don't tell me how I feel. Matt Canseco is . . ." She trailed off, picturing his dark-chocolate eyes, that thick shock of shining hair. She thought about how her heart had leaped every time he gave her that lopsided smile, courtesy of curvy lips.

"You were saying?"

"Matt is a good contact. He knows about all this show-biz stuff, and he can help me learn—and he's fun."

Dash shook his head. "Like I said, be careful."

Her cell phone rang, ending their squabble.

Logan! She grabbed it, telling Dash she'd take it in her bedroom. Before she closed the door and plopped down on her bed, she heard Dash say, "I'll start reading the scripts."

"Logan! I'm so psyched that you called! I have so much to tell you—and we barely got to talk yesterday. I was at a photo shoot; then I had this interview; it's a cover story for *Seventeen*! Cool, huh? Then I got attacked by paparazzi, and then . . ." She stopped herself. Best to leave it there.

"And I guess there was that bar thing afterward, huh?" Logan, who'd obviously read the blog, finally said.

"Kind of," she admitted, "but whatever you read got so blown out of proportion! I had a teensy-weensy bit of wine. And I wasn't personally involved in a fight—"

He cut her off. "Jacey, relax. This is me, remember?

Boyfriend? On your side? You don't have to defend yourself. I saw the pictures. You looked terrified. I wish I'd
been there to defend you."

"Me, too." Of course, unless Logan had pulled up in
the car as Matt had and parted the paparazzi, there was
little he could have done. She flipped onto her back and
gazed at the ceiling. "So I guess everyone at school has
seen the pictures, too?"

"Some kids feel badly for you."

"The fight-or-flight instinct kicked in," Jacey told him
honestly.

"Yeah, I heard who you flew off with!"

Jacey tensed. Should she debunk any rumors Logan
might have heard?

Logan didn't give her a chance. His tone was
starstruck. "That must have been cool. Meeting a movie
star like Matt Canseco! Did he give you any acting tips?"

It hadn't occurred to Logan to be jealous. He'd always
been loyal, even when she was away. In a lot of ways,
Logan Finnerty was the perfect boyfriend. She slipped a
pillow under her head, laced her fingers together, and felt
her body relax for the first time all day.

"So, enough about me. What's new at school?"

He was excited about college, just as she had been.
They'd both chosen to stay in Michigan, he at the

University of Michigan, she at nearby Michigan State. It'd be cool having her high school boyfriend become her college sweetheart.

Before they hung up, she pressed him for some information about the senior play. She'd campaigned for *Wicked* and had wanted to star in it as the green-hued, misunderstood, wicked witch Elphaba, the part Jacey's archrival, Tiffany West, had landed.

"How's Tiffany"—Jacey snickered every time she said the name—"doing as Elphaba?"

"I hear she's good."

That was not the answer Jacey had been hoping to hear. At least Logan's next bit of info was an envy eraser. The class had chosen a date for the senior prom. "It's gonna be late this year, Saturday, June fifteenth," Logan said.

"So, are you asking me?" she said coyly.

"Not yet," he teased. "Not sure how I feel about paparazzi trailing us."

She laughed. "C'mon, you're a lock for prom king. You deserve some celebrity!"

By the time she hung up with Logan, Jacey was feeling much, much better. Relaxed and happy, she drifted off into a nap, dreaming about what to wear to the prom.

It was dark by the time she woke up. A hot shower

totally revived her. And so did the aroma of Asian-fusion takeout wafting down the hallway. Her friends had ordered from Tuk Tuk Thai and were sitting spread out in the living room, eating at the coffee table and watching TV.

Jacey popped her head in. "Any left for me?"

"Of course, Your Crankiness," Dash replied.

Desi was sporting an oversize yellow-and-green-striped wool beanie, which covered her curls.

"That is so Brad-Pitt-at-the-airport-clutching-the-baby!" Jacey squealed. "Where'd you get it?"

Desi had picked it up at a cool boutique she and Ivy had hit that afternoon. Giggling, she admitted, "It was seventy-five dollars—but I *had* to have it."

"Whatever you guys bought, you know it's on me, right?" Jacey said, feeling guilty about her evil behavior earlier in the day.

"Not necessary, you're paying us," Ivy reminded her.

"Plus free rent, an apartment, a car. It's really enough," Desi added.

"Please," Jacey waved them off. "You all deserve combat pay after the last couple of days."

"Well, in that case," Desi mused, "guess I'll keep that killer Tracy Reese dress."

Jacey plopped down on the carpet, pretzeled her legs lotus style, and dived into a bowl of miso soup followed by drunken noodles, *gyoza* dumplings, and chicken pad thai.

"What accounts for this mood swing?" Ivy asked cautiously.

"The nap," Dash said. "And the call from Logan."

Jacey slurped her soup. "There was mention of the prom."

"And so, Logan is back in your good graces, huh?" Dash grinned.

"Like he ever wasn't?" A sudden thought struck her. "What if . . . I don't even want a next movie? Would it be so bad to just go home in a few weeks, after the *Four Sisters* premiere?"

"Yes," Dash said, "it would be so bad. Because while you were sleeping off your irritability, I did a quick read of the scripts Cinnamon gave us. I was just telling Desi and Ives, two are killer, just great, great stories, meaty roles. One's kinda dopey, but I could see how people would like it, and the other would depend on the special effects, so it's hard to say. But sweet Cinnabon did right by you. I'm gonna wear an 'I Worship Cinn' bracelet to our next meeting."

Jacey polished off the last of the noodles. "Okay, Dashiell. Let's hear it."

The first script Dash described was a crime caper called *Jennifer Falling Down*. Dash said it was "about an insecure young girl—a Bridget Jones, Jr.—who gets pulled into a robbery, which becomes a murder. Solving it, and extracting herself, gives her a path to self-esteem."

"Sounds cool." Jacey said. "But if I'm playing Jennifer, wouldn't I be shouldering the whole movie?"

Ivy scanned Cinnamon's notes. "Nope—they're looking at a big male star—someone like Justin or Orlando for the lead."

"Oh, my God, I love Orlando!" Desi exclaimed. "Do that one!"

Jacey agreed. "That's a maybe."

The second choice was *Cosmic Catnip*, a screwball comedy about three couples and their mixed-up cats. Jacey scrunched up her nose. "That's the dopey one, right? Toss it."

"That was my feeling," Dash concurred. "Though Cinnamon's notes said that movies with animals do well. Plus, this one offers a short shooting schedule and an extremely large paycheck."

Script number three, based on the wildly popular book *The Historian*, was Dash's favorite. "It's an adaptation of the origins of Count Dracula and kinda great."

"So it takes place in Romania? Does it film on location?" Ivy asked.

Dash leafed through Cinnamon's notes. "Uh . . . yeah.

For three months. Starting in August."

The fourth was a futuristic fantasy adventure called *Galaxy Rangers*, starring a team of young people, each of them chosen for a specific ability to save the entire galaxy. "Sorta like *Star Wars*?" Desi asked.

"More *Matrix* or *V for Vendetta*," Dash said. "This is the one that depends on the special effects. But the upside is that it's an ensemble piece. You'd be one of the leads, and it's only a couple months of shooting—for which you earn a ton of money! And best of all, it starts in a couple weeks, just before your *Four Sisters* premiere. The timing is perfect."

Chapter Six

If You Were a Tree,
What Kind of Tree Would You Be?

During the first weeks of May, Jacey was the model It girl, obediently spending time with Avery, the media adviser; Brad, her image consultant; publicist Peyton; and Irina, her stylist, the newest addition to Team Jacey. It was all necessary, in her agent's view, to prepare fully for the grueling rounds of interviews and photo sessions Jacey was obliged to do for *Four Sisters*.

The schedule was brutal. For two days, there would be a revolving door of reporters, every half hour for eight hours straight. Minibreaks would be held for meals. At least she'd be ensconced in a suite at the posh Beverly Hills Hotel.

She was all set to answer questions about her movie

character, Ava. And she was happy to share with reporters how she'd researched her character, transformed herself into her. On the advice of her media adviser, she'd come up with half a dozen "appropriate" behind-the-scenes anecdotes, should she be asked. She'd been warned that some questions would turn personal, and she had been coached on the way to answer those. She knew which questions she could be candid about and which Peyton would politely refuse to allow her to answer—so she couldn't, not wouldn't, deal with nosy questions about the debacle at Dungeon, or her run-in with the paparazzi. She was allowed to lie outright when answering some questions, as long as she injected info about the movie into each interview.

It had been decided by Irina, the stylist, that Jacey should look young and hip, but respectful, when she met the press. The outfit chosen was Rock & Republic jeans, woven pink flats, and a T-shirt under a Chanel blazer.

Between the coaching and the couture-ing, she was beyond ready—way more prepared than she'd been for her SATs!

Until the first question.

"Is your name a reference to our Lord?" The reporter was from the *Sentinel*, of Asheville, North Carolina.

Her friends, posted around the suite, were supposed to be quiet, but Desi made a loud smacking noise as she clamped her hand onto her face. Ivy's jaw dropped; Dash chuckled.

Jacey was just plain stupefied.

Peyton politely spoke up. "We're not sure we understand the question."

The reporter replied, "Jacey, J.C. . . . ?"

Oh! She bit her lip so she wouldn't laugh. "My dad's name is Jacob, my mom is Cecile. That's pretty much it."

The reporter's follow-up questions were, thankfully, more routine, and practically identical to the dozens that followed.

Jacey's practiced response concerning her costars was just short of gushing. "I worship their work! They taught me so much, were so gracious to me." She varied the wording and length of her answers, so each writer might come away with a different quote.

Most of the questions *were* about the movie and her character. That was when she came alive. Yes, she certainly had gone back and read *Little Women*, the source material; she had rented DVDs of all the movie adaptations. Although she was all about the version starring Winona Ryder, Claire Danes, and a very young Kirsten Dunst, she totally agreed that this new version would be more relevant today.

There were queries, some nosier than others, about

her personal life. She was careful not to reveal too much about her parents nor pinpoint her actual Bloomfield Hills neighborhood, although anyone who'd watched *Gen Next* had seen videos of both.

The "boyfriend question" she'd been advised to answer thus: "I have a lot of friends back in Michigan, but I'm focused on my career right now."

"It's important," her image consultant had said, "that all your female fans identify with you, and want to be your friend, and that all your guy fans believe they have a chance with you."

She'd protested. "But what about Logan? I already told the *Seventeen* reporter about him. It'll look like we're broken up now."

"Prepare him," had been the highly paid expert's advice.

Grudgingly, Jacey had acquiesced. If Logan was hurt, he covered it well. In fact, he made jokes about being the big secret back home.

"How does it feel to be a role model for all the girls out there who want to be just like you?" one reporter asked.

"I don't think of myself as a role model," Jacey said modestly. "I'm not perfect or anything. If there's one thing I hope I represent, it's 'Totally follow your dream'! Try your best, take every opportunity you can."

"What do you like best about being an actress?"

"It's like shopping, in a way," she said thoughtfully. "Trying on different people. It's cool to lose yourself completely in someone else."

The next reporter declared, "We're on rumor patrol. Let's start with you and Matt Canseco."

Jacey fielded that one easily. "I met him by accident. He rescued me, as everyone knows. That's it. End of story."

"So you didn't go to a club with him?"

"I was at a club. He happened to be there. So were dozens of other people. It was fun. It was cool. I'm having the best time here in L.A., getting treated so nicely by everyone!"

"What's your relationship to Gina Valentine? Rumor has it you two got into it that night at Dungeon."

"The rumor is false," Jacey said, folding her arms, although she'd been told not to. "Gina was at the club, but I never said a word to her."

"What about the rumor that Gina was already signed for the role of Ava when you swooped in?"

Jacey shrugged. "I didn't know anything about that."

Once the reporters understood that they weren't getting any down 'n' dirty details from her, they dropped it and went back to the standard questions. Someone always asked, "What will your next movie be?"

"I've just signed to play the role of Zorina. She's an extremely cool, take-charge, action hero, in *Galaxy Rangers*. It's totally state-of-the-art. It's being directed by a hot new talent, Emory Farber, and I get to start filming next week." She usually ended with one of the following: "I'm beyond pumped," "I'm so excited," or "I can't wait to get started!"

By the end of day one, she felt like Robo–It girl, divulging the same info over and over again. Her face hurt from smiling, her eyes watered from all the photo flashes, and her hand cramped from signing so many autographs "for my daughter—she's such a fan; she voted for you every week!"

Appearing friendly, excited, articulate, as if each question were being asked for the first time, was hard work!

But it was the last question of the day that really threw her. "Who is the blogger?" The reporter from *The New York Post* leaned in close. "How does he know everything about you, and why is he slamming you?"

Peyton fielded the question. "Jacey wishes she knew. She'd like to communicate and understand why this person is being so mean and unfair to her. If she's done anything to offend him or her, she'd like to find out what it is and possibly even set things right. But right now, she's completely in the dark."

It was evening by the time Jacey was relieved of press duty and got to go home. Dash, Desi, and Ivy were figuring out a fun plan for the night. As long as it didn't require any talking or smiling on her part, Jacey wanted to join in.

The posse debated movies, restaurants, clubs—or, they could stay home, with some greasy pizza and the season six DVDs of *Sex and the City*.

Any of those scenarios would have been okay with Jacey. The only one she'd have nixed was the one waiting for them as they turned off Barham Boulevard in to the driveway of the Oakwood Apartments complex.

A horde of fans, armed with signs, greeted them as if they were heroes returning from war. Or the winners of the Super Bowl. Or Jessica Simpson. Or . . . the winner of *Generation Next*, Jacey Chandliss.

Young teenage girls mostly, with a sprinkling of guys, lined the road from the entrance all the way to their apartment door. The first sighting of the Jeep seemed to flip the switch marked: SHRIEK! LOUDER! The sound was not unlike that of a pack of caterwauling hyenas—or, as Dash snarled, "K-Fed dueting with a sack of angry kittens."

Dozens held up signs proclaiming their devotion to Jacey; some proudly displayed the number of times they'd voted for her on *Generation Next*. All wanted autographs, photos, face time with their idol.

It was the paparazzi scene all over again—unexpected and unwelcome, but necessary to deal with.

This time, however, they did know how to deal—and they knew that, no matter what, Jacey had to.

"We love you, Jacey!"

"Can I get an autograph? Please!"

"We've been waiting for hours," a group shouted in unison. "Please pose for a picture with us!"

"I'm your biggest fan!"

The posse sprang into action. Desi dialed their personal 911s—Cinnamon and Peyton. Ivy carefully parked the car. Dash opened the passenger door and scrambled up to the roof, where he could be seen by all as he addressed them.

"This is so cool of you guys to come out here. It's like a surprise party! Jacey is beyond grateful to have such amazing fans. She's had a long day, but she's happy to come out and talk, sign some autographs, but we've got to do this in an orderly way. So if you could form two lines . . ."

Desi hung up the phone and turned to Jacey and Ivy. Through clenched teeth, she gave them the bulletin from Cinnamon. "While we were at the Beverly Hills Hotel doing press, turns out the blogger struck—finally getting something right this time. Our address."

Jacey stayed in the car, opened the rear window, and leaned out as Dash led the fans up to her. She signed dozens of autographs, smiled for cell-phone pictures, and personally thanked as many fans as possible. After a while, the authorities—in the welcome form of Peyton and Cinnamon, plus the unwelcome form of the building manager—showed up.

The former, armed with preautographed head shots of Jacey, were able to satisfy the fans who hadn't gotten up close and personal with their idol.

The latter—the building manager—demanded that Jacey vacate the premises. *Permanently.*

"We're evicted?" Ivy said incredulously. "It's not our fault all these kids showed up here."

"Can you legally force us out?" Dash wanted to know.

The manager *could*—thanks to an obscure clause in the rental agreement about causing a riot on the property— and *did*. He wanted them packed and out the next day, or sooner. "Tonight would be good," he grumbled before turning away.

Cinnamon immediately booked them into the Peninsula Beverly Hills hotel. She consoled them. "Forget about this dump. You put in a tough couple of days. Go pamper yourselves in the coolest hotel in town. We'll figure out what to do tomorrow. But tonight, use the spa—it's *fabulous!*"

They needed no further encouragement to hang a U-ie and get their butts over to the way-famous Peninsula, where Cinnamon had reserved each of them a luxurious private suite—all expenses paid, courtesy of her agency.

A delicious room-service meal, a dip in the rooftop pool, and a trip to the spa—the agent was right, it was *fabulous!* They slept well that night.

Good thing, too. The next day started early. "It's the only time I could squeeze in," Cinn explained, sweeping into Jacey's suite at 7:30 a.m., trailed by Brad, the hulking image consultant.

Over breakfast—fresh California fruit, flaky croissants, granola, yogurt, cappuccino, and cocoa—Cinnamon said, "You're going to buy a house. With a big, strong, security gate. We just need to decide where. Location is everything—that's why Brad's here."

Granola bits tumbled out of Jacey's open mouth. "You're kidding, right?"

"I never kid so close to dawn."

"But I'm not even eighteen! I can't own a house," Jacey blurted out.

"And yet, your bank account, and current circumstances, say yes, you can." Cinnamon, chic in a Diane von Furstenberg wrap dress, settled comfortably into a cushy club chair in the living room and explained that the *Galaxy Rangers* deal she'd negotiated called for a fantastic paycheck up front, with bonus points on the "back end."

No one needed an English-to-showbiz dictionary to understand the message: Jacey was going to earn millions for her *Galaxy Rangers* performance—in only a few months of filming.

Desi's jaw hit the ground. "She's a millionaire?"

Cinnamon ignored the question. "You cannot live in a place where fans can storm your apartment any time that ridiculous blogger decides to out you."

"But, a house? That's so permanent. I'm not sure if I'm actually staying—"

"Whaaat?" Cinnamon cut her off. "You have a movie to shoot and a premiere to attend, not to mention the gigs I'm lining up for you."

"What Jacey means is . . ." Ivy stepped in. "It's all new to us, and overwhelming."

"Will it be in cash?" Desi had not gotten past the paycheck.

"Is it okay if we take a little time to think about it?" Dash asked.

Cinnamon traded a see-what-I'm-up-against? look

with Brad, who jumped in. "Your agent has your best interests at heart, Jacey. You really should follow her advice. The only question you need to ask yourself is, are you making the commitment everyone thought you'd already made when you won *Generation Next*?" he asked, not unkindly.

"It's time to trade up and put down roots. Let Hollywood know you're here to stay," Cinnamon said brightly.

"Well, a house is something we can always sell," Ivy mused. "That is, if we decide . . . if Jacey decides that being a homeowner isn't something she really wants at this stage in her life."

"Settled!" The sound of Cinnamon triumphant was a beautiful thing. "Now all we need to decide is the right neighborhood. That's the reason I dragged poor Brad out here. He's the expert on coordinating your image with your residence."

A vision of a speeding express train zoomed through Jacey's mind—she was hanging on to it by her fingernails.

Cinnamon turned to Brad. "Where should we start our search?"

"Hollywood!" was Desi's suggestion, not that anyone had asked her opinion. "Why not live in the heart of it all?"

Brad was too scandalized to speak.

Cinnamon wrinkled her nose. "Too tawdry."

"Bel-Air," Dash suggested.

Brad shook his head. "Too young. No one under a hundred lives in Bel-Air."

"The beach? Malibu?" Ivy offered. "That's a cool area, and I'd love being by the ocean."

Cinnamon nixed that one. "Too far from the studios. Besides, the beach is out of your price range."

"What about the Hollywood Hills?" Desi wanted an address with the word "Hollywood" in it, Jacey thought, grinning.

"Too artsy," Brad scoffed.

Jacey tried to contribute to the conversation, suggesting the only other neighborhood she'd heard of.

"Eagle Lake?"

"Are you kidding?" The *eeew* on Brad's face made him look as if he'd just sniffed squirrel poo. "That's not even in the Zone. And don't even think of anywhere in the Valley. Sherman Oaks. Woodland Hills. Burbank. Encino. We're not going there."

The foursome exchanged identical confused expressions.

"What's wrong with right here? Beverly Hills?" Cinnamon asked brightly. "We'll do the Flats, which she can afford. It means, rich, hip, young, but classy, Rodeo

Drive. It's total American-aspirational."

"It's what?" Desi asked. They'd lost her at "the Flats." Which turned out to be shorthand for the low-lying, residential part of town.

Ivy lit up. "That's near the Golden Triangle, all the snazzy shops!"

"Beverly Hills . . . probably not a bad idea," Dash mused. "Probably be easy to sell if . . ." Cinnamon's look stopped him.

Jacey knew two things about Beverly Hills: its 90210 zip code, where TV's Brenda, Brandon, Dylan, and Donna once resided; and this bizarre little show she'd caught once on TV called *The Beverly Hillbillies.* She banished the second image from her head.

Cinnamon, excited now, leaned forward in her chair. "Beverly Hills is its own municipality within Los Angeles. There are two areas—the Hills, which is outrageously expensive, and not really for you, and the Flats, between Santa Monica and Sunset Boulevards, where there are a variety of homes and prices, many behind secure gates. It's easy to get anywhere from there."

"And Jacey gets to boast a Beverly Hills address," Brad added, "without having to count on her next four paychecks."

Jacey's stomach tightened at that.

The approaching panic must have shown on her face, because Cinnamon said, "Here's how we'll do it. Ivy and Dash will do the heavy lifting—I'll set them up with a *fabulous* realtor—all you have to do is work on *Galaxy Rangers* and get ready for the *Four Sisters* premiere."

That, Jacey could handle.

Jacey Blindsides Press
About Her Boyfriend[s]!

During her so-smooth-you'd-swear-it-was-scripted round of interviews for *Four Sisters*, Jacey barely blinked when answering the "boyfriend" question. She said she was single. Whatever happened to Logan, the "true love" she blabbed about all during *Generation Next*? Kicked to the curb already? Has Matt Canseco replaced him? Or is it her new *Galaxy Rangers* costar she's gone gaga over? So many boys, so little truth . . . ah, Jacey, don't you know it's a tangled web we weave when we practice to deceive? Maybe getting evicted was karmic backlash.

Chapter Seven

Galaxy Rangers, Take One!

"Oh, babee, babee . . ." A whistle greeted Jacey on her first day of filming *Galaxy Rangers*. She'd spent the morning in the wardrobe trailer, had her hair and makeup done, and she was now transformed, at least on the outside, into her character, Zorina.

To say she didn't love it was Understatement City. That Bozo look at the *Seventeen* photo shoot? She was feeling nostalgic for it.

The whistler, Adam Pratt, was her costar. She'd met the pale, good-looking, blue-eyed blond during rehearsals. Though *Galaxy Rangers* was Adam's first movie, Jacey thought he'd be okay to work with. Now she wasn't so sure. She hoped his whistled compliment on her skintight pink-and-blue bodysuit (festooned with strategically placed silver zigzag lightning bolts) could be chalked up to first-day-on-the-set nerves. Then he came close and winked. "Love that outfit. It's all you, starlet-girl."

Instinctively, Jacey backed up, hoping he'd take the hint. He didn't, so she looked for something to occupy her. Spying the crafts services table—showbiz-speak for the catering cart—she headed toward it, grabbed a corn muffin, and stuffed it into her mouth.

Adam shook a finger at her. "Sure you want that? You'll get crumbs all over your lovely ensemble."

"Then I'm sure." Jacey swallowed a huge piece.

Adam, suited up in his own abominable silver costume, was playing the role of Zartagnan, Zorina's partner in fighting crime.

Galaxy Rangers took place "sometime in the future" and centered around three pairs of teens who patrolled the universe, ferreting out evildoers, including the baddies who'd murdered the scientist parents of each of the teens.

"They're the peace activists of the future," was Cinnamon's bright-eyed take.

The big twist was that one of the teens was double-crossing the others, working with the bad guys. Zorina, the heroine, would expose them and foil their plan.

Squirming in her costume, under the lascivious eye of

her costar, Jacey had to remind herself of why, exactly, she'd chosen to do this movie. Mentally, she ticked off the reasons.

Timing. The schedule was short—it started shooting now, in May, and ended in early August, keeping alive the choice of returning home after the summer.

Convenience. The movie lot was just outside of Beverly Hills, something she'd appreciate when her call times were for early morning.

Her agent. Cinnamon believed *Galaxy Rangers* was a worthy follow-up to *Four Sisters*. Although it was special-effects dependent, it'd be Jacey's first action-hero role. "It's zippy and hip; it coordinates with your image," said Cinnamon. Which sounded more like an ensemble than a career move.

Jacey considered the cast: the six main roles were played by actors best known for having appeared in TV shows like *The O.C.*, *One Tree Hill*, *Gilmore Girls*, and *Girlfriends*. If they'd chosen it, the movie couldn't suck too badly, right?

And Jacey had to be honest with herself. The money was great. Okay, *that* was big. She'd be earning a crazy-sick amount, enough to pay her entire college tuition and to buy the coolest outfits for a baby brother who was on the way. There'd be money to buy an excellent prom dress, plus killer designer clothes to wear to the *Four Sisters* premiere.

And there would be money for a place to live in Beverly Hills.

Though for the past couple of weeks, living at the five-star Peninsula hadn't been too hard to take!

"What a sacrifice!" Logan had laughed during the previous night's phone call. "You'll get spoiled at that place. Room service every night, maids cleaning up after you, your every need taken care of."

"Well, not *every* one," she'd countered coyly. "Sweet dreams!"

Jacey and Logan talked and/or texted every day. She'd been trying to convince him to come to L.A., to be her arm candy for the *Four Sisters* premiere.

Now, she checked her Coach watch, a seventeenth-birthday gift from her mom. Hmmm . . . it was around lunchtime in Michigan. Good time to sneak away from Adam the Annoying for a little Logan-lobbying.

"The premiere's gonna be killer!" Jacey told Logan. She could hear a group of Logan's buddies in the background, at Wolverine Pizza, a favorite lunch spot. "Think about all the stars who'll be there. I'll introduce you to Julia Barton, Kate Summers, and Sierra Tucson. C'mon, how sweet will that be?"

"The only star I'm interested in is you!" Logan teased her.

"You're cute, but I'm serious. C'mon, what's to stop you from coming out here for a long weekend? I'll make it worth your while."

"You know I can't," Logan said with a sigh. "That weekend won't work for, like, a million reasons."

Jacey heard raucous laughter in the background as Logan listed his reasons: "I have to study for advanced placement tests in language arts, chem, *and* Spanish. If I ace those, I start college with a bunch of credits. *That's* sweet!"

"Can't you study on the plane?" Jacey pleaded. She was really missing him.

"Saturday is graduation rehearsal," Logan said. "I can't miss that."

"Who's at lunch with you?" Jacey suddenly asked, hearing a familiar female voice call, "Logan—your pizza's getting cold."

"The usual crew," he answered. "Bailey, Zeke, Emma, Mike . . ." Something or someone distracted—or tickled—him, and he started to laugh.

"What's so funny?" Jacey asked, a wave of homesickness washing over her.

Logan was still laughing. "Nothing. Beth's just being obnoxious."

Beth. As in, Beth McKay, best friend of Tiffany West? Jacey pressed her lips together, to keep from asking if Tiff was there, too.

"I gotta book, Jacey, but remember, watch the mail. A certain invite is on the way!" Logan clicked off.

Jacey knew that Logan was talking about the prom, and she was excited. But she couldn't understand why he wouldn't miss rehearsal for a gala Hollywood premiere. Did he really prefer that to one night of magic?

Was there a backup date for her? she wondered. Maybe . . . Matt Canseco? He was notorious for refusing to attend high-wattage premieres, awards shows, anything he considered "Hollywood trappings." And like he'd agree to be *her* date? Right. Dream on, Jace. She hadn't even heard from the rebel rouser in weeks. The only place they were linked was in her blogger's imagination.

Resignedly, Jacey strolled back on to the set.

"Ah, I see my two stars are here, right on time, and from the looks of you, ready to start shooting!" The director—short, squat Emory Farber—had arrived, a dog-eared script jammed under his arm, a *Lord of the Rings* baseball cap on backward, headphones around his neck, and a walkie-talkie in his hand. It was the official uniform of Hollywood directors.

They were on Stage 16, one of dozens of identical

stucco soundstages that resembled warehouses. Inside each one, a TV show or movie was being filmed.

Emory waddled across their set pointing out carpenters, electricians, and other tradespeople working to create the three-walled rooms they'd be shooting in. He introduced Jacey and Adam to the crew—the people behind all those names that would roll down the screen at the end of the finished movie. Included were several assistant directors, camerapeople, grips, best boys (who could also be girls), and lighting and sound team members.

A script prompter was on the set at all times in case someone forgot a line. So was a woman whose entire job consisted of "continuity"—making sure the actors looked the same in sequential scenes. In all, there were dozens of people, and their official uniform seemed to be jeans, sneakers, T-shirts, and baseball caps.

There were many people wearing microphones and holding walkie-talkies. They all looked busy, setting up cameras, arranging lighting, and positioning the large boom mics around the set like giraffes.

Finally, Jacey, Adam, and Emory reached their destination, the section of the set where they would film the first scenes. Here there was no scenery at all, save for a huge green backdrop. It reminded Jacey of the *Seventeen* photo-shoot backdrop, but this, Emory explained, had another purpose. The special green screen was there so that when they were done filming, the F/X folks could add the whiz-bang, computer-generated special effects.

Act one, scene one, introduced Zorina and Zartagnan, patrolling the galaxy on a pair of futuristic scooters. Only, there weren't any actual scooters. They would be added later, via computer. Jacey and Adam, donning "asteroid-repellent" driving gloves, had to feign gripping handlebars. A humongous fan was turned on high, blowing the actors' hair back to simulate a windy day in outer space.

In other scenes, they'd pretend to ride horses, or Harleys, tricked-out cars, and spaceships. The Galaxy Rangers had all manner of transport for their various missions.

The third AD directed them to their exact places, and, along with the second AD, demonstrated how they'd pretend to be on scooters while talking, ducking cosmic rays and asteroids. Zartagnan was to be portrayed as a show-off. He'd be swerving, racing, even performing intergalactic wheelies!

Before they began, Emory reminded them that Zorina, a smart, savvy, take-charge girl, wasn't fond of Zartagnan, whom she considered a blowhard and braggart.

And, where, Jacey snickered inwardly, would the acting part come in? Jacey knew her lines, was prepared and ready, but Zartagnan—that is, Adam—had questions. "Shouldn't I be riding ahead of her?" and "Shouldn't I be the one who points out that something's strange about the star in the distance?"

Jacey turned away so they wouldn't see her rolling her eyes. Adam was already campaigning for her lines. Whatever. On her first film, *Four Sisters*, and even on *Generation Next*, Jacey had learned what it meant to be a pro. You didn't waste time on the set. You did the part as directed. If you had an issue, you had a private meeting with the director. Emory, however, was patient, and willing to indulge Adam. "We'll try it both ways," he agreed.

Finally, Jacey heard the words she'd been patiently awaiting: "And . . . action!"

"Beautiful night, beautiful teammate." Zartagnan was flirting with her, but Zorina, engrossed in her own thoughts, merely nodded.

"Is something wrong?" he asked.

"Your powers of perception are admirable, Zartagnan." Jacey decided not to play it straight, as she had in rehearsal, but add an edge of sarcasm. Since no one said, "Cut!" she figured it was okay. "What isn't wrong? We've lost our families. . . ."

"I know," Zartagnan agreed. "But we are sworn to police the skies above Jupiter tonight. We must be vigilant."

She turned to him, pleading with her eyes. "Don't you want to find out what really happened?"

"We know what happened. The laboratory blew up."

"But why? Haven't you ever wondered? Our parents were scientists. They wouldn't have made a mistake that could lead to catastrophe."

"So you're saying maybe it wasn't an accident?"

"Once again, Zartagnan, you astonish me with your powers of perception." This time, she punctuated the line with a friendly little laugh. Jacey didn't think Zorina disliked him that much—yet.

"And . . . cut! That was da bomb!" Emory raved. "What a great shoot this is going to be!"

Then he snapped his fingers. Three ADs came running. "Zorina's hair," Emory said to them. "It's not working for me. Tell the stylist to add some spikes. It'll symbolize her edge. I want her edgier in the next scene."

At the break, Jacey gratefully retreated to her superdeluxe silver Airstream trailer. The first thing she did was to nearly clock Dash, who did a double take when he saw her costume. "I didn't know Pink Power Ranger and Oscar the Grouch had a daughter!"

"They had a thing?" Desi tugged at her curls, confused. Snuggled on the designer couch in the trailer's living-room area, she'd been flipping through a fat issue of *In Style*, sipping from a cold can of soda. Everyone looked cool and comfortable, relaxing in the trailer.

Unlike Jacey. "It's hot under the stage lights," she whined.

Ivy turned the AC up, and Desi fished her an ice-cold bottle of water from the full-size fridge in the Airstream's kitchen.

"If you're tired, go into the bedroom and take a nap," Dash suggested. "Maybe catch *Oprah* on that big-screen TV hanging over the queen-size bed." Jacey was the only actor on the movie to have scored such lush digs. It impressed everyone.

The star decided to stretch out on the couch. She slipped a pillow under her head, kicked off Zorina's silly, silver, futuristic boots, and propped her feet up on Desi's lap. The water refreshed her, as did the plate of berries Ivy offered.

Jacey regaled her friends with a description of her morning, mimicking Adam, mocking the dialogue, aping the way she and Adam had pretended to be riding invisible scooters with the wind blowing. She had everyone cracking up.

"Sorry you decided against *Cosmic Catnip* now?" Dash quipped.

"Maybe I should have thought more about *Jennifer Falling Down*," Jacey said. "That was a great script."

"But that wasn't gonna start filming until October. You weren't sure you wanted to stay that long," Dash reminded her, tossing blueberries in the air and catching them in his mouth.

"Speaking of home—*homes*, that is," Ivy said as she booted up the laptop, "are you up for a virtual tour?"

While Jacey had been in rehearsals for *Galaxy Rangers*, Ivy and Dash had been trolling for lodging.

"How many do you have uploaded there?" Jacey asked.

"We narrowed it down to seven or so," Dash replied. "Let's see if anything turns you on. They're all appropriate for your image, Your Divine Wholesomeness."

"All are close to major shopping, excellent restaurants, salons, spas, gourmet shops, all the major necessities of life," Ivy detailed as she clicked on the first one.

"They're all near Rodeo Drive," Desi put in. "Where the big stars shop."

As if on cue, there was a knock on the trailer door. It was an unexpected visitor from a galaxy she wished would stay far, far away: Adam Pratt.

Without a formal invitation, her smiling blond costar came in—and he was all about the Airstream trailer.

"Whoa! I knew you snagged plush quarters, but, man, this is sweet. The rest of us are sharing digs."

"You thirsty? Want something cold?" Desi offered.

"Thanks," he said. "Just came to tell you we're needed on the set." Adam tried to take her hand. She managed not to let him, realizing even so that that would hardly discourage him. Adam wanted something from her. She just wasn't quite sure what.

jaceyfan blog

Jacey Kissin' Costar?

You read it here first! She can deny it all she wants, but I happen to know that Adam Pratt paid a private visit to Jacey's dressing-room trailer! And from what I hear, the talk, when they *were* talking (!!), was all about places to live. Together? Jacey's movin' fast, boys and girls—but fret not, your secret source of all things Jacey (that'd be me!) can keep up.

Methinks *Galaxy Rangers* is gonna be worth watching for! And not just for the plot!

Chapter Eight

Primp My Premiere

"Hollywood, make way: a new starlet is born. Jacey Chandliss is here to stay."

"Where's that one from?" Jacey asked excitedly. It was early evening, and the group was holed up in Jacey's plush suite at the Peninsula.

"Variety online." Cinnamon, on speakerphone, was reading them advance reviews for *Four Sisters*. Studios often invited selected reviewers to prescreen movies in the hopes they'd spread positive word of mouth. Mission accomplished!

Generation Next *got it right: Jacey Chandliss* is *America's newest star!* gushed moviemaven.com.

A starlet with talent? How often do you see that?

Cameron, Scarlett, and Kate, watch your backs!
declared buzzometer.com.

Aintitcool.com urged its readers, *If you want to witness true talent, do not miss her performance.*

Cinnamon, beyond pumped, had her assistant, Kia, forward the advance buzz to top producers, directors, and casting execs, raving, "This couldn't be better if we'd written it ourselves!"

Did we? Jacey mused. Nothing would surprise her.

"Whether they were paid to write those reviews or not—and I vote for not—" Ivy opined, "it doesn't matter. Like Cinnamon said, 'it's not how good you really are, it's how good they *think* you are.'"

Most days, Jacey felt confident about her performance.

Most nights, she woke up in a cold sweat, visited by the "what-if" fairies.

What if when Four Sisters *comes out, I get crappy reviews? Or the movie tanks? What if it's as laughable as* From Justin to Kelly? *What if I don't live up to all the hype? What if I go from a shooting star to a falling star?*

"It's just as easy to think positively as it is to torture yourself," Dash said when she confided her fears.

"Thanks, Dr. Phil."

The phone in Jacey's suite rang. Dash picked it up. "Torture Chamber." He paused. "Okay, send them up."

"Send who up?"

"Your stylist hath arrived, Empress Worry-wart, and she's brought a couture coterie. Apparently, an entire ensemble-toting entourage has come with."

The premiere of *Four Sisters* was going to be huge. Jacey needed to be ready. What would Irina choose for her to wear? Would it be hideous? Like the milkmaid outfit from the *Seventeen* shoot? Or, to borrow a Cinna-mism, would it be "fabulous!"? Would she wear sparkly, expensive jewelry? Would Logan show up after all, as a surprise? What shoes? Could she even *walk* in Jimmy Choos?

And, once the movie began, could she sit still in a theater filled with stars, critics, reporters, producers, directors, and random VIPS, watching them watch her—on a ginormous screen? Would her head look Bratz size? Would people in the front rows look up her nostrils? What if people laughed in the wrong places? What if people laughed at her?

Irina, trailed by assistants pushing coatracks packed with dresses, and others hauling trunks filled with shoes, jewelry, bags, and accessories, swept into the large suite. As if they had rehearsed, the assistants—some of them, it turned out, designers' reps—pushed the furniture against the wall, creating a large space in the middle of the room. "The dresses," Irina explained, "need room to breathe. To be displayed to their best advantage."

This was about the dresses? Jacey had had the mistaken idea it was about her.

Desi snagged a prime spot on the floor, ready for the *Project Runway* fashion show.

Ivy pored over the racks of dresses, excitedly reading out the designer names on the tags. "Gucci! Prada! Versace! Armani! Aläia! Oh, my God, Jace, Stella McCartney! You're gonna wear one of these!"

"No way they'll fit!" Jacey said nervously, absently running her hand along her curvy hips.

"They *make* it fit." Desi, devoted reader of *US Weekly* and *In Style* magazine, fancied herself knower of all clothes tricks.

Irina confirmed that seamstresses were ready to nip, tuck, or let fabric out as soon as they decided on something.

"The concept," the stylist said, "is about radiance. We will choose a couture look that will define young, hip, and—"

"Wholesome, I know," Jacey interjected.

"Maybe we can sneak a little sex appeal in," Irina said with a wink.

Jacey grinned. Irina was okay.

Over the course of several evenings, Jacey channeled her inner Tyra—if you could picture the host of *America's Next Top Model* a shrimpy five feet three inches and more tomato-round than string-bean skinny. What did she learn, slipping in and out of these scarily expensive frocks? They were *so* not in J.C. Penney-land anymore. Not even Nordstrom's, Neiman's, or Bloomingdale's. She knew nothing about fabric or stitching or even (don't tell anyone) what "haute couture" meant. But you didn't have to be Heidi Klum to see that these ensembles came from another zip code altogether.

First off the rack was a J. Mendel pleated, satin-faced, V-neck, chiffon dress, with a hand-painted tulle underskirt. Jacey thought it was flattering and pretty, but Ivy scrunched her nose. "Looks like your slip is showing."

A form-fitting, spaghetti-strapped Molly & Jack dress covered in pink-circle sequins was then nixed because "you look like you're covered in dollar slots," Desi so delicately told her.

After about a half-dozen try-ons, Irina suddenly declared, "Wait. Stop everything. I've got it. We should play up your eyes, your most arresting feature—and we'll go with hues of blue or violet."

The declaration sent the designer dudes scurrying to

pull out appropriate frocks.

Jacey twirled and sashayed across the room in form-fitting and flowing halter-necks, V-necks, sleeveless and strapless dresses in shades of periwinkle, sapphire, lavender, and indigo by designers she'd heard of, like Gucci, Stella McCartney, Chanel, Max Mara, and Marc Jacobs, and some she had not—like Proenza Schouler and Viktor & Rolf. She felt like a princess, albeit, after a while, a pooped princess.

By the third straight night of the fantasy fashion show, her friends agreed: "Just pick something!"

On the fourth night, she did. Irina showed up with two finalists.

The first was a flirty, sparkly Missoni spaghetti-strap frock in shades of purple, lilac, and plum. The outstanding feature was its awesome bikinilike top, covered in sparkly Swarovski crystals.

"It's young, it's darling, and it's a hint of sexy," the stylist determined. "You wear your hair long, shiny, wavy, just brushing your shoulders. We pair it with strappy silver sandals—you'll do pale lilac nail polish—a one-strand diamond tennis bracelet, and delicate drop earrings. This look says, 'I'm not trying to overshadow anybody, but I am so radiant and girlie you can't ignore me.'"

Her posse gave the dress a unanimous thumbs-up.

Jacey liked it, too. She felt floaty, lighter than air, as if she could twirl in the dress all night long. Her parents would approve. And yet it allowed for some cleavage. Logan would be sorry he had missed it. If he missed it. And if Matt Canseco happened to see her picture, maybe he'd come up with a more appropriate nickname than the one he'd given her that night at Dungeon—Dimples.

"Now," Irina said, "I want you to try on one last dress. It just came this afternoon. It's completely different from anything else we've seen. It's daring and risk-taking. Are you ready?"

It was definitely different. Midnight blue, it boasted a strapless, form-fitting bodice that stopped at the waist. The skirt, borderline mini, was ruched, made entirely of black taffeta ribbons. She could see it on a tall, slim model. Yet in a strange way, it worked for her.

"Well," Jacey said, "this is either gonna be a showstopper or a shoo-in for the 'When Bad Clothes Happen to Good People' column."

Irina closed her eyes, seerlike. "I envision this with stacked-heel black sandals, diamond drop earrings—and nothing else. Your hair in an elegant updo, your shoulders and neck in the spotlight. It makes a statement."

"What's it saying?" Dash was doubtful.

"It's saying, 'Watch out, world, Jacey Chandliss is here

to stay.' It's saying she's fearless, a trendsetter, one of a kind, fabulous!" Cinnamon had arrived at their suite exactly on cue!

"So you think I should wear this? You didn't even see the other one," Jacey said to the agent.

"Sweetie, you can have them both and decide at the last minute. But in my mind, there's no contest. This is your first premiere. You steal the movie. Now, go steal the limelight."

"I can't see! I'm blinded!" Jacey panicked. In the glare of giant klieg lights, spotlights, and a zillion camera flashes all going off at once, Jacey couldn't see a thing. What an entrance! Her first time on the red carpet, and her main emotion? Terror. So this was why stars wore dark shades, she realized. Forget snob appeal. They simply wanted to see.

Dash, in an excellent Armani suit, took her arm and guided her onto the red carpet. "You're doing great," he whispered into her ear.

"I can't see," she whispered back.

"Your eyes will adjust, relax. Until then, let me do the seeing for you. Just smile and act dazzled."

"I can't breathe, either." The bodice of her dress was so tight she didn't need a bra.

"Breathing's overrated." He powered her forward.

As for the bulb-bottom skirt? Long strides were not an option. "I can't walk. I'm gonna wobble, teeter, fall on my face," she complained to Dash.

"Just hang tight."

Hanging on to Dash was precisely what she'd been doing. Exiting the limo, going through the metal detector—something they don't show on TV!—and now, making her entrance on the red carpet.

Desi and Ivy were right behind her. As soon as they emerged into the glare of the spotlight, Desi began to hyperventilate. "Oh, my God, there's Ty Pennington! He's my idol!" She held up her camera-phone and snapped away. "I see Ryan Seacrest! And Kristin from the original *Laguna Beach*! She totally stole LC's dress!"

Cinnamon had told them this premiere was going to be big and splashy. For once, the agent had understated it.

Fabulosity reigned!

Velvet ropes separated the throngs of fans lining one side of the red carpet from the press, who lined the other. All vied for the attention of the stars, and no one would be disappointed tonight.

The glitterati, as Dash dubbed the pretty people, had turned out in droves for the premiere. The red carpet was riddled with stars, one more bronzed and Botoxed than the next, accessorized with dates, mates, publicists, entourages, and well-rehearsed sound bites. This was Hollywood wildlife in its natural habitat, providing a feeding frenzy for the press, fans, and paparazzi.

Peyton—svelte, chic, cool, and coordinated—suddenly materialized, ready to lead Jacey through her press and photo paces.

The big photo op was the one featuring the four stars of *Four Sisters*. It had tickled Jacey that this shot had been carefully choreographed—that is, negotiated—ahead of time. Not only who'd stand where, but what color dress each of them would wear. "Not too matchy-matchy, not too clashy-clashy," Peyton said in a singsong voice.

"Is that really necessary?" Jacey had asked Peyton. "Deciding days before who stands where?"

She got her answer the hard way.

The shot, which would land in all of the major magazines, had to showcase Julia Barton. The biggest name in *Four Sisters*, she'd already starred in several hit movies and was considered the next Cameron Diaz. It didn't hurt that Julia, a smart, slinky blond with swimming-pool blue eyes, resembled Ms. Diaz. For the premiere, she wore a vintage Dior gown that hugged her in all the right places.

Kate Summers, a Nicky Hilton look-alike with masses of dark curly hair, showed up in a bold, canary-yellow,

Gucci halter dress. She was to stand next to Sierra Tucson, swathed in bronze Versace.

Jacey, shorter by several inches than the rest of the cast, was placed next to Sierra. Although she wore stacked heels, so did her costars. Theirs were higher.

Height gave the actresses an edge, which they used to their advantage. Just as the camera clicked, Sierra stuck her elbow out, totally obscuring Jacey's face!

Jacey was astounded.

"What was that about?" Cinnamon stormed over.

"Oops, sorry," the actress said with a phony smile. "Didn't realize they were just about to shoot."

Peyton demanded a do-over.

This time, Sierra tilted her head back in Jacey's direction—just enough to block Jacey's face. Again.

Steam was coming out of Peyton's ears. A quick crisis-management conference between Sierra's handlers and Jacey's straightened it out. Sort of. The shot was done again—but this time, Jacey stood next to Kate.

But Kate insisted on cocking her head slightly to the left, to show off her "good side."

Her hair covered half of Jacey's face.

Desi's fists were ready, Ivy was livid, Jacey was furious, and Peyton was royally pissed.

Cinnamon had to calm them all down. "They're jealous

that you got all the advance buzz," she whispered. "If they can knock you out of the shot, they will, but don't worry. Nothing they can do will change how great you are in the movie. Let it go."

Julia decided to play the equalizer. She asked the photogs for one more shot—a "candid"—of her with her arm around Jacey; they looked like two extremely dressed-up girlfriends.

That was when Jacey got proof of another showbiz saying: "The bigger the star, the nicer they are."

After that strange red-carpet scenario, Jacey got to greet her old friends, the team from *Generation Next*, all bursting with pride.

"You're making us look good," Sean, the host, whispered to Jacey as their photo was taken. "Showing the world we really did pick America's Top Young Actor."

"Let's see the movie before deciding," Jacey replied modestly, squeezing his hand.

Just then, Adam Pratt, who would probably have come to the opening of a can if he could have had his picture taken, materialized and planted an unwelcome kiss on Jacey's cheek. "What an exciting night for you! Thanks for inviting me." Then, turning to a nearby shutterbug, he said, "I'm Adam Pratt, and I have the honor of costarring with Jacey in her new movie." The photog snapped away.

Peyton rescued Jacey. "*Access Hollywood* is ready for you now."

The entertainment show had a surprise for Jacey. They pointed out something she hadn't yet noticed. Dozens of young fans were holding up a huge banner: CONGRATS, JACEY, FROM YOUR CREW AT BLOOMFIELD HILLS HIGH! WE'RE SO PROUD!

Logan? Was Logan there? Jacey's heart raced as she attempted to—momentarily forgetting that she couldn't—bound over to them. Turned out these were seniors from Hollywood High, who'd been asked to represent her Midwestern homies.

"That's so sweet!" Tears welled up, threatening to ruin her makeup, as the cameras rolled. She wondered who had organized this surprise. One girl offered a bouquet of roses, saying, "These are from your parents."

A reporter spoke into the microphone: "You're seeing an *Access Hollywood* exclusive! Jacey Chandliss, surprised and delighted by the show of support from her hometown. Jacey, how 'bout a shout-out to the folks at home?"

Jacey smiled through her tears. Over the lump in her throat, she quietly said, "You guys are the best. I hope I do you proud—I miss you." She touched two fingers to her lips, then to her heart, and then held them up to the camera, all the while thinking that maybe this had been Logan's idea.

She was about to thank the *Access Hollywood* people for facilitating the touching surprise, but they'd moved on to Julia, whose date, rock star Rudy McDaniels, had just shown up. The fans went wild. They dropped her banner.

The red-carpet scene was like a revolving door: handlers, cameras, and press moved one celebrity out, another in. There was much jockeying for position to interview the "biggies." These included stars from all of Jacey's favorite TV shows and movies, and a sprinkling of pop and hip-hop stars. There were also random party-peeps who had never met a camera they didn't like.

Every once in a while, Jacey stole a glance at her costars. Julia made it look so easy. Even the backstabbing Kate and Sierra acted as if they weren't scared, as if their stomachs weren't twisted into a hundred pretzels, and as if their feelings weren't hurt when they were dismissed because a bigger star had eclipsed them.

Jacey stopped to talk to *Extra*. Desi had lobbied for an up-close with its rock-star host, Mark McGrath; she got a peck on the cheek and a picture. She was in heaven.

Later, Peyton quietly mentioned that it was very uncool for her to be taking pictures, which was Desi's cue to do it only when Peyton's back was turned.

Spying a slim celebutante in a backless sheath, dash sidled over to Jacey and whispered, "Does that dress make her spine look fat?"

Jacey cracked up. She squeezed Dash's waist and gave her escort a peck on the cheek as they reached the end of the red carpet. Time to go inside the theater. Time to find out if all the hype were real—whether people still rooted for her.

She took a deep breath. She could do this.

The Arclight was one of L.A.'s newest and flashiest theaters. In the heart of the newly revamped Hollywood and Vine neighborhood, across the street from where the Academy Awards were held, the venue had comfy stadium seating and a surround sound system. By the time Jacey and her friends got inside, it was packed to capacity.

Beyond the stars and their entourages, everyone who worked on the movie had been invited. Jacey recognized dozens of crew members and their families. Cinnamon, seated behind Jacey in the VIP section, leaned over and pointed out studio bigwigs, producers, directors, casting execs, and movie reviewers—any of whom could have a big effect on Jacey's career, if they liked her performance—or, not that the agent had to say it, if they hated it.

Jacey refused all offers of snack or drink. She didn't trust her stomach. Dash squeezed her hand, which reminded her of something. "Can I check my BlackBerry?" she asked. Dash had been holding it for her, since it didn't fit into the teensy, bejeweled, Judith Ripka purse she had.

There were two new messages. *Break a leg, baby—I know you're gonna be great! Love, your Logan.* She smiled, feeling warm all over.

And this one: *Dimples, good luck. Dungeon later?* It was unsigned.

She melted.

At the "Please turn off all cell phones, Sidekicks, BlackBerrys, and beepers" announcement, she reluctantly handed her device back to Dash. The lights went down. Jacey took a deep breath.

This was it.

Chapter Nine

Kisses 'n' Kudos: the Afterparty

As soon as the end credits rolled, the entire audience was on its feet, applauding wildly, whistling, and hooting. As the names scrolled down the screen, it was like a contest to see who'd elicit the biggest, loudest, noisiest cheers.

First, the director's name appeared, and her cheering squad clapped, howled, and stamped their feet. Then the producers' posses gave major noisy props to their peer-peeps. And so it went, through the entire crew, everyone's friends and supporters trying to outdo everyone else's. Even the assistant to the assistant grip had brought a crowd to cheer him on.

The crazy clamor took Jacey back to her *Generation*

Next days, when the cheering competition had been between Angie's Angels, Carlin's Crew, and Jacey's Posse. Except that then there hadn't been big stars doing the screaming.

The most earsplitting raves were reserved not surprisingly, for the cast. Julia Barton got the above-the-title star billing and the cheers to match. Then Kate's and Sierra's names came on the screen accompanied by clapping, whistling, and *whoo-hoo*ing. Jacey's name was not there among the actresses who played the sisters. The next credits to roll were those of the male leads: Chad Murphy and Teddy Granger. A tiny spark of panic went off in her brain: had they forgotten—

And introducing Jacey Chandliss as Ava.

The entire theater went into wild overdrive. The screams of Dash, Desi, and Ivy were off the chart. They squeezed her so hard it was a good thing she hadn't eaten!

Cinnamon, aglow, winked and Jacey suddenly got it. Cinnamon had negotiated this special billing for her. It was a surprise, and a really big deal. In Hollywood, it proclaimed the fact that she had arrived.

Jacey was floating on air. She loved her agent. She loved her publicist! She loved her friends! She was gonna buy them all presents!

★　★　★

The afterparty started up on the glitzy balcony of the Arclight's café, and that was when Jacey drained her first glass of champagne. She toasted everyone!

The scene was one "Oh, my God—there's so-and-so!" moment after another. A blurry, star-filled whirlwind.

Cinnamon and Peyton guided Jacey to an S-shaped blue couch—one of two that bracketed the room, which was full of bistro tables and bars. Always thinking, always jockeying for position, Jacey's agent and publicist claimed the primo spot for her to receive well-wishers. Dozens descended.

These people had seen the movie, seen her work. If they were all saying how great she was, and if, deep down, she kinda knew she'd aced it . . . then, wow—it must be true.

All around her were an exceptionally well-dressed mix of celebrities and their handlers, a sprinkling of select reporters, plus assorted "industry-ites," as producers, directors, casting agents, and entertainment lawyers were categorized. They were all blowing kisses, plying her with kudos and offers of "meetings or lunch, dinner, or power breakfasts."

It was as if they were welcoming her into their circle. They were the cool kids, she was the new kid. And suddenly they were saying, "You're with us, now. We just voted, and you're in."

Lindsay Lohan came up to her! Jacey was floored when the singer-actress told her what an amazing talent she was—and suggested working on a movie together sometime. Sisters Hilary and Haylie Duff offered props; even Kelly Clarkson was there, telling her about Mood, a hot club she and the posse ought to check out.

While Jacey was holding court, her friends helped themselves to the sumptuous buffet and toted appetizers over to her. Specialties of the house included chicken black bean chili, sweet-corn tamales, and juicy miniburgers.

The martini of the night was named Four Sisters, in honor of the movie, and it was made with four distinct ingredients. Jacey had no idea what they were, nor did she care. The drink, like the night, was sweet and went down smoothly.

"Now," Cinnamon instructed, "it's time for you to make the rounds. There are some very influential people here tonight. You should meet them."

As her agent led her through the crowd, she overheard snippets of exchanges. "You were spectacular!" "Your best performance ever!" "No way, it was all you!"

Finally, Cinnamon found someone she'd been searching for. "Michael, I'd like you to meet Jacey Chandliss."

The big-name director sandwiched Jacey's hand in his, showered her with compliments, and suggested a meeting. "I'll have my people call yours."

Jacey bit her lip so she wouldn't giggle. If one more cliché was added to the pile, would it tip over?

Next on Cinnamon's list of people to suck up to was a megaproducer. He gave her props and said, "I'll set you up with one of my staff. We'll talk!"

There was another person at the party whom Cinnamon didn't point out: a skinny, gawky guy she recognized from that night at Dungeon. Noel Langer—the "next big thing" who was directing Matt's movie, *Dirt Nap.*

She started to head over to him, but in what was fast becoming an annoying habit, Adam Pratt was in her face again. Worse, he had brought reinforcements—his date, Tara, who was her own special brand of stupid. Sloshed, she bleated, "You're so lucky. Wish I had a blog like yours. It means you have a stalker!"

Jacey didn't know how to respond to something like that.

"Having a stalker means you've arrived! Between a stalker and gay best friend, girl, you're the man!"

Cinnamon quickly had Ms. Hammered-head removed.

"Ignore that," she advised her suddenly nervous client. "Comes with the territory. And after tonight, our territory will be quite fertile. This," she motioned around the room, "is what's called a lovefest. You cannot imagine how many more offers I just got for you!"

"Everyone wants an interview." Peyton sidled up to them. "I heard from the bookers for *The View*, who would like you to come on; same thing with *Conan*. I'm waiting for *Oprah* to call back."

Desi trotted over, leaned her head on Jacey's shoulder, and slurred, "I'mmm liking Champlain."

"Champlain is a lake," Jacey said, correcting her. She impulsively hugged her. "Champagne is what you're guzzling—lots of it, my friend."

Ty Pennington, star of *Extreme Makeover*, came into Jacey's line of vision. Feeling bold, Jacey marched Desi over to Ty, extended her hand, and said, "I'm Jacey. This is my best friend Desi—she's your biggest fan."

She trotted giddily away. This was what royalty felt like: everyone fawning over her, and she could wave a magic wand and introduce Desi to her idol and trade banter with major directors, producers, and stars!

She didn't want to go back to her corner of the couch. She wanted to take all this in, snap a mental photo that could never, ever fade.

Even though he was probably asleep, she texted Logan: *Wish you could've made it. It's so unreal without you.* Then she scanned the room. She checked to see if Matt had made the scene. No sign of him, nor of his posse.

Ivy strutted up to her, sipping on a long straw, which dipped into a frozen daiquiri. "How much are we loving this party?"

Jacey pointed to Noel Langer, who was across the room in an intense convo with a man she didn't recognize. "That's the guy from Dungeon, who's directing Matt's next movie. I want to meet him, but Cinnamon vetoed it. Do you think it'd be a real breach of etiquette if I just, you know, did it?"

"Oh, cuz, it's all about you tonight," Ivy encouraged her. "You're golden. He probably wants to meet you!"

Jacey began to walk over. She was two feet away, behind them, when she overheard Mr. Langer and his companion talking about . . . her?

"So, what's your take on the newbie, the reality show winner?" The question came from Noel's friend.

"Jacey Chandliss? Hard to tell from that movie if she's got any real chops," Noel said. "Could just be a lightweight who lucked into a great role."

Jacey stood rooted to the spot, her jaw hanging open.

"I wouldn't go out of my way to take a meeting with her," he said. "Even if she does have talent, they're grooming her to be the next glam girl or weenybopper—not exactly what I'm looking for."

Jacey was astounded, wounded, and dazed. If she had a tail, it would have been between her legs. She scurried back to her corner of the blue couch.

Tears had just started to cloud her eyes when someone tapped her on the shoulder. Startled, she whirled around and found herself staring up into the swimming-pool-blue eyes of Julia Barton.

"Got a sec?"

Jacey's heart leaped. In all the huggy hoopla, not one of her costars had come over. "Oh, my God, I so wanted to say how amazing you were in the movie—I just got swamped over there," Jacey burbled.

"Watching you brings back memories," Julia said wistfully. "Just be ready. Today, a lovefest; tomorrow, the claws will come out. People will be jealous, and they'll show it in ways you cannot imagine. Don't let it get to you. You did a tremendous job in this movie, you're the real deal, a real talent, and if you want it, you can have a huge future in this business. Keep your friends close, your enemies closer, and your 'frenemies' closest of all."

Jacey thanked her, even though she didn't understand some of what Julia said. She had about a million questions. How could she tell who was blowing smoke up her tush, and who—like Noel Langer—had "reservations" about her? What had it been like for Julia when she'd first arrived? What should Jacey be looking out for? But Julia had caught sight of someone she knew, and she dashed away. Suddenly the president of the studio, Rex McCann, was on a bullhorn, summoning the crowd. He asked that everyone quiet down and gather around. Jacey rushed back over to her friends.

The very first reviews, the ones that would be in the next day's papers, had been e-mailed to McCann—he read them directly from his BlackBerry screen. *"Julia Barton dazzles; Kate proves that she's a bigger talent than her TV roles would have you believe; Sierra, this is your comeback. As for luminous newcomer Jacey Chandliss, a star has definitely arrived."*

Jacey found herself gulping for air as she squeezed Dash's and Desi's hands. This was surreal. Rex continued reading: *". . . Her blue eyes are like magnetic orbs that pull the audience in to Ava's story, sometimes putting it on a par with, if not eclipsing, the other story lines. Jacey doesn't give her character merely a voice, but a soul."*

Whoops of joy erupted, the loudest emitted by Team Jacey. Jacey wanted to take that sentence and shove it at Noel Langer!

McCann quieted the room down and went on reading. *Four Sisters* had gotten four stars, or the equivalent—from every reviewer who'd been at the premiere. It was going to rock the box office. Estimates were through the roof.

After the cheering and patting on the back subsided, he had another announcement. As a token of his gratitude to the stars, and on behalf of the studio, there would be a special gift waiting for each of them at home.

Desi wanted to rush back to find out what the token was, but Jacey, still bathing in the glowing reviews, air kisses, and kudos, was in no real hurry to leave. She'd just been welcomed into a very elite club. Forget Noel Langer. Her membership had been earned.

It was well beyond four in the morning when the limo delivered an exhausted but exhilarated posse to the Peninsula hotel. As they pulled in to the circular driveway, they saw something glinting under the portico lights: a brand-spanking-new silver Mercedes convertible with a giant white bow on top.

They stumbled out of the limo to get a better look. Written on a banner attached to the bow were the words *Congratulations, Jacey! With love from your* Four Sisters *family.* It was signed by the producer, the director, and movie-studio execs.

The friends were too stunned to speak.

Jacey just stared at the car. What planet was this where people gave away hundred-thousand-dollar luxury cars just to say, "Thanks for a job well done"?

"I've never been this close to a Mercedes," Desi exclaimed, running her finger along the driver's-side door. "It's so . . . cute!"

"It's so . . . new!" . . . a stunned Ivy put in.

"You don't have to keep it," Dash, ever the voice of reason, said. "If you don't want to."

"I shouldn't keep it?"

"Are you nuts?" Desi said. "It's a gift. They'll be insulted if she doesn't keep it. And how cool will it be to bop around town in this?"

"What happened to 'American cars only'?" Dash reminded them of the unspoken credo they—and nearly everyone they knew—had. "We're from Detroit. We drive American cars."

"I don't think we're in Detroit anymore, Toto." Ivy continued to circle the Mercedes.

Jacey's mind was clouded. She couldn't think, let alone make a decision. The hotel's valet made it for her. "Why don't you all go up to your rooms? We'll take care of the car for you tonight."

As the elevator let them off on the penthouse floor,

the scent of roses suddenly overwhelmed them.

A trail of blushing pink petals had been sprinkled in the hallway, leading from the elevator past Desi's room, past Dash's, past Ivy's . . . to Jacey's door. The foursome exchanged glances. Another token of appreciation?

The lights had been dimmed in Jacey's room. The trail of rose petals continued, leading from the suite's living room into the bedroom. On the night table sat a huge bouquet in a gorgeous vase.

Her heart raced. Who? Who had done this? Not the studio. This was too personal.

A card was attached to the flowers. *Will you be my date for the most important night of my life, the Bloomfield Hills senior class prom? Your biggest fan, Logan.*

All the air went out of her, and Jacey dropped to her knees. She gathered up a fistful of the soft, scented petals, pressed them to her heart . . . and started to sob. This had been the most perfect day of her life. She could not have scripted it better.

jaceyfan blog

Frock Flop!
Jacey Blows It at Premiere!

What was she thinking? The dress Jacey chose for her glitzy red-carpet debut made her look more like "snowman goes black tie" than a sweet starlet! Between her round face, round top, and extremely round rump—all she needed was a carrot for a nose and a porkpie hat to complete the look.

Hips don't lie, but Jacey—why, why, why?

Blame it on first-night jitters, fire the stylist, fire your gay best friend—but no one should have allowed you out in that abomination. And speaking of blame—where was the mirror? That dress is made for Keira, Uma, Mischa, or Nicole. Notice, no J.Lo, Shikira, Beyoncé, Britney, or . . . you. Get my drift, curvy one?

I'll grant you props on the screen time and the credits (nice move, agent!), but the ensemble? You blew it.

Chapter Ten

When Posses Collide—
Jacey's House Party

On a lazy early Sunday evening the following week, Jacey looked down from the rooftop terrace of the house she'd just bought. This was Beverly Hills, her new neighborhood. Nothing about it looked, smelled, or felt like home.

Here, the boulevards were wide, but pin-drop quiet. Every so often a car went by, slowly pausing at the intersection. Here, the streets were pristine, lined with flowering jacaranda shrubs and palm trees so tall and slinky they looked like an anorexic chorus line of feather dusters.

The houses, one more glorious and architecturally dazzling than the next, were gated, but sat practically atop one another. So many rich people, jammed into such a small area.

And not a single human being in sight.

"No one walks in Beverly Hills," the realtor had advised them. "Even if you're only going a few blocks, you drive. That's how we roll here."

Desi had taken that advice to heart. Right now, she was out for a spin in Jacey's shiny new Mercedes, theoretically on a food-and-drink-gathering mission, but more likely bopping around town, showing off.

Ivy and Dash had finally strong-armed Jacey into looking at houses. All the McMansions she saw had been amazing, but she couldn't have pictured herself living in any of them, until this one.

A sprawling colonial on North Cañon Drive, between Sunset and Santa Monica boulevards, this house had beautiful olive trees lining the cobbled driveway, all the way from the gate to the front door. Out back, there was an Infinity pool, a huge hot tub, and a cabana area. It looked like the plush resort at Torrey Pines.

Each of the five bedrooms boasted a private balcony and what Ivy, wide-eyed, called "drive-in closets." Jacey's cousin was tickled by the Great room, with its vaulted cathedral ceiling and a pitlike covered fireplace in the center of the room built to look like a snazzy campfire.

Instead of logs, it was surrounded by Armani Casa sofas.

"Hollywood's interpretation of camping out," Dash had snorted. He was impressed with the upstairs library, filled with "real books, not props!"

Desi was head over heels for the fully equipped game room.

What had sealed the deal for Jacey was the rooftop terrace, a small sundeck with two outdoor recliners and a snack table, enclosed by a waist-high brick wall.

Jacey called dibs on it. This would be her private place to read, write, text, or—as she was doing now—to ponder, dial it down, hop off the Jacey Express, and hit the MUTE button.

All the reviews for *Four Sisters* were in, echoing the early buzz, heaping hyperbolic praise on Jacey's perform-ance. It was terrifying and exhilarating at the same time. Awesome reviews brought huge audiences—many who'd voted for her in *Generation Next*—making *Four Sisters* number one at the box office for several weeks running.

She was officially Hollywood's It girl now.

"Never believe your own press," Peyton was quick to advise. "Don't get high on yourself when everyone's fawn-ing over you. And don't get down on yourself when they—and they will—trash you."

Jacey wondered if she should take all this praise

seriously. Or should she assume it would all end tomorrow? Would she return to Bloomfield Hills at summer's end, go off to college, or not?

She inhaled. The breeze was citrus-scented. She gazed at the slinky trees, the colorful flower beds that had been randomly placed atop the parapet enclosure, the orangey pink sun setting in a pale blue sky.

Hearty laughter bubbled up from downstairs. Dash and Ivy were embroiled in a diving-and-splashing contest in the backyard pool.

"Come on in, movie star," Dash called up to her.

Jacey smiled.

She *was* a movie star.

A movie star who had politely asked for—not demanded—and gotten time off to attend the prom with Logan. Which made Logan one extremely excited boyfriend.

And the downside was what?

Okay, she'd overheard one person voice reservations about her talent. There was the gnawing worry that her performance in *Galaxy Rangers* might prove him right. Yes, there were some people jealous of her (*see*: Kate Summers, Sierra Tucson, Gina Valentine). And the blogger, an ever sharper thorn in her side.

This time, it'd pricked, and drawn secret tears. The

blogger had gleefully trashed her outfit, her figure, even her friends. It was just plain mean. And hurtful. Still, no one knew who the blogger was—but woe betide him if Desi, Ivy, or even mild-mannered Dash found out! There were scores to settle now.

But in this moment, 7:45 p.m. on a Sunday evening in early June, it was *all* good.

A squeal of tires jolted her out of her reverie. She jumped up. Below, a gleaming red Viper, with a license plate that read INDISPRT, had stopped inches from the security gate, followed close behind by a silver Escalade.

What was up? She had company? When she realized *who* was outside her gates, Jacey's heart raced. How did they know? Ivy! Her cousin must have invited them, as a surprise. Cupping her mouth with her hands, she called out, "Look who's here—there goes the neighborhood!"

Matt Canseco shaded his eyes, looked up, and shot her a mischievous smile. "Yo, Dimples, wanna open the gate, or should we take a chance, find out who'd win in a Escalade-Viper smack-down with your flimsy front gate?"

Jacey hurried to meet them.

Ivy and Dash, thick towels wrapped around their wet bodies, ushered the guys into the house.

Matt and his friends had brought a couple of six-packs and a chilled liter of wine. Jacey went to put everything on ice while her friends scurried upstairs to change.

When she emerged from the kitchen, the guys had settled themselves in the den. Wearing a tight black T-shirt over faded jeans and Tods loafers without socks, Matt looked hot. He ran his fingers through his thick dark hair and scoped out the room. "Sweet crib," he said appreciatively.

"Thanks. It is kinda cool," Jacey agreed, trying for nonchalant, but falling short at lame.

"Who's thirsty?" Dash asked as soon as he returned. "We've got what you brought, plus Desi's out getting more."

Emilio asked for a beer; Rob, Aja, and Matt settled for iced tea and bottled water. Meanwhile, Ivy put music on.

"All this stuff came with the house?" Rob kneeled in front of the fireplace pit. "You didn't have to hire a decorator?"

"We just moved right in," Jacey acknowledged. "It was pretty smooth."

"Come on, we'll give you the grand tour," Ivy said. Her head of wet waves dripped onto the tight top she'd put on.

Jacey hoped Matt and his friends didn't think they were showing off. Reluctantly, she tagged along, letting Ivy give the commentary on the kitchen, den, library, and bedrooms. Finally, they got to Jacey's room—and her bathroom.

"This bathroom rocks!" Emilio exclaimed.

"It should," Ivy pointed out. "It's a spa."

"I sit corrected." Emilio, in a wrinkled white T-shirt with the sleeves cut off, pushed his shaggy hair out of his eyes and parked himself on the marble steps that led up to the Jacuzzi bath.

Everyone laughed, and Jacey relaxed, noticing that Emilio kept stealing glances at Ivy. And her cousin was sneaking looks right back.

The bathroom was enormous, tiled in dusty tones of marble, glass, and granite. A working fireplace was set into one wall. The Jacuzzi tub, big enough to fit two comfortably, had a working TV built into a protruding corner of the frame.

"This is *sick!*" Rob crowed, hitting the remote to change channels.

"I bet she bought this entire house just to watch Jacuzz-TV," Matt cracked.

Jacey pursed her bee-stung lips coyly. "Maybe."

Ivy grinned mischievously and flung open the glass shower doors. "Wait'll ya see this." She leaned in to turn on the water, and it came shooting out of six nozzles at once. "Pivoting body sprays! You can point it at your head, shoulders, midsection, front, back, legs. You can set it to soothing or pulsating . . . ."

"Two people could get really . . . *clean* in it." Emilio met her flirtation, and raised her an innuendo.

Jacey checked out Matt's reaction. His eyes twinkled.

"Down, guys! Cool yer jets!" Dash quipped, pretending to fan himself. "Gotta see the game room. *It's* wicked."

Dash wasn't exaggerating. The room that had delighted Desi so much was a gamer's paradise. Three working pinball machines had been installed, plus the latest video game consoles: Nintendo's Wii, PlayStation 3, and Xbox 360. There was a poker table, a pool table, a giant plasma TV, a stereo—even a retro neon jukebox skirting a polished wooden dance floor.

"I'm moving in!" Aja exclaimed. "I challenge anyone to a game of Space Invaders!"

"Bring it," returned Dash, claiming a primo spot in front of the pinball machine.

"I can take you both!" bragged Rob, positioning himself next to them. "I'll play the winner of your first game. When I crush him, I'll take on the other one."

Emilio's flip-flops made a thwacking sound as he bounded over to the jukebox, put on some club music, and motioned for Ivy to join him on the dance floor.

Which left Jacey, Matt, and an awkward silence. Jacey

was not a big gamer. She suspected Matt wasn't, either. For a minute, she couldn't think of anything to say. So she blurted out, "I wonder where Desi is? She should've been back by now. We won't have anything to eat until—"

Matt seemed amused by her floundering. He folded his arms across his chest and took in the entire room. "So, it looks like you decided to stay."

"Huh?"

"Stay. Here in L.A. Like I predicted. Moved from the temporary apartment to a house. You just did it faster than I thought you would."

"I had to buy the house, everyone said so. Even my parents."

"Yo, I'm not putting it down. Don't be defensive."

"I'm not being defensive," she countered. "But you're movie star-boy, you must have a house, too."

"Nope. I rent. I'm not into owning things."

"What do you do with all the money you make?"

He shot her a look.

Jacey wanted to disappear. How rude had that comment been?

"You saw my ride," Matt joked. "All my money's tied up in my car."

"I can't believe I asked that," she said. "I'm sorry."

Matt nodded toward the pool table. "You play?"

"A little." *Verrrry* little.

Matt removed the pool cues from the wall holder. "I'll rack. You break."

Gripping her cue, Jacey watched Matt fit the balls inside the triangular plastic holder. "Go ahead, break," Matt told her.

She searched her memory, trying to call up a movie scene with pool playing. Had there been one in *Pretty Woman*? Her stepdad had *The Color of Money* on DVD . . . she tried to remember what the positions were. She laid the pool cue on the table and leaned over it.

Matt laughed.

Busted!

"Wanna learn?" Matt asked. "Be a shame to own this vintage table and never use it."

Which was how, without meaning to, or trying to, or wishing to, Jacey ended up pressed against Matt's chest, inside his strong, sure arms as he draped them around her. She was conscious of Matt's being shorter than Logan, of how her head seemed to fit neatly in that soft spot just under Matt's collarbone.

He placed one arm over hers and taught her to put the narrow end of the cue between her thumb and forefinger, pressing the other fingers down on the table for support. He demonstrated pulling the cue back, then shooting it forward toward the ball.

She was hyperaware of his leaning into her, the feel, and sound, and aroma of his breath close to her ear—if he had been Logan, which he wasn't, this might have been the moment he'd have playfully licked her earlobe, placed his lips on her neck. If he had been Logan, the lesson would have been over about now.

"So you want to call the ball you're aiming for," Matt was saying. "One that's not too close to any of the others, but nearest to a pocket. Ready?" He helped her draw her arm back and . . .

"No! Not the black one! Any one but the black one!" He smacked his forehead with the heel of his hand. "Sorry, I forgot to mention that part."

"How about you shoot a few, and I'll watch?" Jacey suggested.

He talked while he played, explaining his every move. She sneaked peeks. Sure, she'd seen him in movies, had partied with him at Dungeon, but up close in better lighting, he was different—if possible, even better looking. Jacey watched him and wondered what accounted for his bad-boy reputation. There was a lot she did not know about Matt Canseco.

She became aware of how noisy the game room was. Pinball machines—Rob, Dash, and Aja had three going at once—were dinging and clanging, the music was turned up, and Emilio and Ivy were dancing, singing, grinding. She and Matt were talking, playing a friendly game of billiards. Accent on the friendly, she reminded herself. She definitely had a boyfriend. Rock solid.

She could have a friend who was a boy. She could even be attracted to someone else. Hello, Matt was a movie star! If Logan had been in a room with a hot movie star, he'd have been attracted to her, right?

Emilio and Ivy were working up a major sweat dancing. It was Ivy's idea that they all cool off with a dip in the pool.

After the boys changed into bathing suits they had borrowed from Dash, Matt did a running dive in, splashing everyone within five feet of himself. Rob raced Aja for the diving board, while Emilio, holding hands with Ivy, jumped into the deep end, where they stayed tangled together.

Aja soon cajoled Dash to dive in, and after a while they were doing laps. Jacey, remembering that the sound system was also connected to the backyard, ducked inside the house to put on a mix of tunes. It wasn't until she got back outside that she realized she'd made it kinda loud.

The next thing she knew, she hit the water hard, smack on her belly. Hair was in her eyes, chlorine in her mouth and up her nose. Someone had snuck up behind her and shoved her into the pool!

Jacey broke the surface, spitting water and venom. "That was not cool! Which one of you—?"

She stopped in midrant. A trio of scantily dressed girls were laughing heartily, pointing down at her. Gina Valentine and her pack of big-haired hyenas? What were they doing here?

Everyone was shouting as Jacey—really childishly—tried to splash them hard as she made her way to the rim of the pool and hoisted herself out of the water.

Dash, Ivy, Emilio, and Aja quickly followed, their faces registering shock at the party crashers. Gina wore sprayed-on booty-call shorts, a cropped top, and high-heeled flip-flops. Her girls Marina and Trish, in similar getups, were beyond thrilled with themselves.

"Got your ass!" Gina hooted, taunting Jacey. "Got you good!"

Jacey folded her arms over her bikini top and spat back, "What are you doing here?"

"This is a private party," Ivy declared, trying to sound threatening while holding up her top, since her straps had fallen down.

"I was invited," Gina said casually.

"By who?" Dash demanded.

Matt? Had Matt invited her? Why would he do that?

After that unpretty moment in Dungeon, Jacey had assumed she'd never see this she-bully again. How had Gina turned up in her own backyard?

"Word gets out," was Gina's reply. Meanwhile, she lowered herself into a lounge chair and wiggled out of her shorts, revealing a thonglike bikini bottom.

"What's to drink?" Trish asked.

Jacey's mind raced, but the questions came from Dash, who fired them at close range. "How'd you know where Jacey lives? How'd you get through the gates? What kind of nerve do you have, busting in here like that?"

Gina remained annoyingly blithe. "Like I said, word gets out. There are no secrets in this town, you should know that. Besides, I could've sworn I was invited. I must've lost my e-vite."

"Now, you can just get lost," Ivy said. "Pick up your stuff and leave."

Matt and his crew hadn't said a word. Jacey checked them out. Matt was leaning against the side of the pool— a look of amusement on his gorgeous face. Emilio remained obliviously playful, kicking a ball.

Rob. Had to be.

Dash had come to the identical conclusion. But as he went to confront Matt's prickly-haired bud, Jacey blurted out, "You know what? You're welcome to stay. All of you."

"That's mighty righteous of you, Sista," Gina said with a smirk.

Ivy and Dash were openmouthed, but Jacey had made up her mind. "Let's get back to our game."

It was awkward, but before long, they had a serious water-volleyball game going, with five players to a side. No one was taking any prisoners. There was dunking, slamming, punching, and spiking—it was a miracle no one got hurt.

When Jacey and Matt rotated so that they were side by side, he slid his arm around her waist and playfully pulled her toward him, whispering, "So how come you didn't kick her ass out of the place?"

Jacey let out a long sigh and uncurled herself from his arms. Because it was obvious to her that one of his friends, if not Matt himself, had invited her. Because, really, what damage could Gina do to her? Julia Barton's words of wisdom kept ringing in her ears. *Keep your enemies close.*

Someone had turned the music up even higher. So when a Beverly Hills cop showed up at her backyard fence, Jacey assumed they'd gotten a complaint.

"You better come out front," the patrolman said. "We have a friend of yours."

Sobbing hysterically, arms and legs bruised, with a bandage on her forehead, Desi sat on the front step.

"Oh, my God! Des, what happened?" Jacey screamed, as she sprinted to her friend, everyone else following at her heels. "Did anyone get hurt?"

Desi tried to explain, but her blubbering was incomprehensible. It was Dash who made Jacey understand, by physically forcing her to look up. In the driveway, next to the police cruiser, sat a tow truck.

Dangling from the hook on the end of it was a mashed Mercedes convertible.

Jacey's Wild House Party
Raided by Cops!

New car smashed to smithereens! Jacey and bad boy Matt Canseco—canoodling in the pool! Has America's sweetheart gone to the dark side?

The angel-baby star of the number one movie in the country is doing some serious partying and acting out! Among her guests at her private house party were bad boy Canseco and his cronies, including troublemaker Gina Valentine.

But it was a member of Jacey's own posse, Desi Paczki, who decided to give LL a run for her money as queen of the bad drivers! How plastered must she have been when she ran the $200,000 luxury car up the sidewalk on Sunset Boulevard, right into Will Rogers Park—smashing into the famous statue?

Why is Jacey surrounding herself with all these bad influences? Is this the little girl we sent to Hollywood to do us proud? And there's more: I hear there are problems with *Galaxy Rangers*. Between ego clashes and plot holes, sounds like Jacey's second movie is headed for the crapper. That'd be enough to make her miserable!

Chapter Eleven

Retail Therapy, Including the Hunt
for the Great Prom Dress

Jacey was not miserable. She checked her Sidekick: nope, no misery on her schedule today. Between work on *Galaxy Rangers*, shopping for a prom dress, and a spin-control interview with *US Weekly*, she couldn't have fit self-pity in even if she had wanted to.

Which she did not, mainly because Desi was okay. And that was huge, she reminded herself, as she perched on the armrest of the couch in her Airstream trailer, sipping a Perrier. What if her friend had suffered serious injuries driving her car? Then Jacey could have made a case for misery. And guilt. But Desi was okay. The seat belt and side air bags had warded off serious injury. And Matt's fawning all over Desi last night had helped bring about a speedy recovery, too. As soon as they'd gotten the wounded bird into the house, Matt had gone all Dr. McDreamy on her, consoling her, hugging her, stroking her hair.

Tears had flowed from her big, sad eyes as Desi whimpered, "I killed Jacey's car."

"No one cares about that," Matt had assured her. "It's bad 'car-ma.' Get it? Good. Now, forget it."

Matt had been right—the car had wowed Jacey, but she didn't really care about it, never even drove it.

As for Matt himself? How could Jacey be jealous of the attention he paid to Desi?

And yet . . . she hated every second he had spent next to Desi. And she hated herself for feeling that way. The bloggerazzi had spread the rumor that Jacey was into Matt. She was definitely not. Not that way, anyway. She already had a boyfriend, and as soon as filming was over, she was all about finding a killer prom dress for their special night.

It was Monday. Prom celebrations in Bloomfield Hills began Friday. Jacey was leaving on Thursday. She *had* to get a move on. And it wasn't as if her personal stylist was going to tote racks of designer dresses to her house for a high school prom!

Then there was the late afternoon interview and photo session with *US Weekly*, offered up by Peyton to cap the damage on Jacey's Pool Party Palooza, as it was being tagged in the tabloids.

Already, Jacey had had to field countless phone calls and text messages from home about it. Her parents were worried; her agent was foaming at the mouth; and her friends from home actually believed what they'd read! So naive! Even Desi finally knew better than to believe what blogs and tabs printed!

It was when she thought about Logan that her heart really sank. He'd tried not to make a big deal of it, but he was obviously unnerved by reports that she'd invited Matt to a private party at her house. Something totally innocent, something she had no reason to feel guilty about— something that would have stayed that way if everybody hadn't found out. Thanks to the Desi debacle, everyone had.

The paparazzi, she'd learned, had police scanners. When the cops went to a celebrity's address, shutterbugs were usually in hot pursuit.

There was a knock on her trailer door. "It's open," she called.

"They're waiting for you on the set," the AD said, popping his head in the door.

"Be right there."

Adam Pratt was on her like white on rice the second she got to Stage 16. "See what happens when you hang out with *that* crowd? Are you *trying* to out-tabloid all of Hollywood?"

Jacey ignored him and took her spot in front of the cameras, poised to work.

"And," Adam continued, "how come I wasn't invited?"

"Action!" Emory called out.

She and Adam shifted into their characters.

This time, they were supposed to be on patrol in a spaceship. Zorina was at the wheel, while Zartagnan behaved like a grumpy passenger.

"Where are you going?" he demanded. "This isn't the way to Jupiter's fifth moon."

"See that motorcycle parked over there?" She motioned to a crater. "Zaftiga's."

"Your point?" he asked.

"What's she doing in the Grissom-Carter Crater? It's a known hideout for the Zod-Pod. I'm going to find out."

Zartagnan shook his head. "Listen to yourself. You were wrong when you tried to infiltrate Mercury, when you thought Zook was betraying us, and you're wrong about this, too. All is peaceful now."

"'Now' being the operative word," Zorina said,

stubbornly steering the spaceship toward the crater. "Wanna bet it won't be so peaceful tomorrow?"

"You're being paranoid. We shouldn't be spying on Zaftiga, or anyone. I don't understand what your problem is."

"You, you're my problem," Zorina said, a little too forcefully.

"Cut!" The director called her on it. "Banter, Zorina! You're supposed to be trading banter—not barbs. Remember, by this point, you're not-so-secretly attracted to him."

That, she thought to herself, would take a way better actor than her!

"And, again . . . action!"

"You, you're my problem." This time, she deleted the intensity.

"Cut!" Not good enough. "Flirt with him," Emory commanded.

"Emory!" she whined, breaking her own rule against contradicting her director publicly. "My character is supposed to be freaked out right now, sure that something bad is imminent, focused on finding out what it is. Why would she be flirting?" This was just one of the many things about the script that made Jacey uneasy.

Her question earned her twin frowns, from Adam and from Emory. Should she continue to fight? It was only one inflection in one line. Whatever. She did the line as directed.

"I have an idea," Zartagnan suggested. "How about we knock off early, and head for the Café @ Venus. We can kick back, relax."

Zorina let out a sigh. "Fine." She paused, then swung the steering wheel right toward the crater. "After I check out what's Zaftiga's doing there."

"Zorina! You're looking for something that isn't there."

"Looks can be deceiving. Zar, there's more going on here."

"Even if you're right," Zartagnan conceded, "who are we to do anything about it?"

"The only ones who can."

"Cut! That was great, just great!" Emory raved.

Adam was suddenly unconvinced. Why, he wanted to know, was his character so stubbornly dim-witted? Why shouldn't he be as proactive as Zorina?

Jacey could have told him, "That's the part you took. If you change him, you change the movie."

"Can you believe it?" Jacey was steaming. "Adam is demanding reshoots!"

"Who is he to demand anything?" Ivy, at the wheel of a newly leased Ford Explorer with tinted windows, had picked Jacey up from work. They were headed for the stores. Desi had recovered sufficiently to tag along.

"My point exactly." Jacey, in the rear seat, folded her arms. "And get this. Emory—Emor-*on*—agreed with him. Set reshoots up for next weekend."

"That's the prom!" Desi, her head still bandaged, exclaimed. "You can't be there."

"My point exactly," Jacey repeated. "Which is what I told them."

"What'd they say?" Ivy asked.

"Don't know, don't care," Jacey said breezily. "I left. Emory promised me the time off—from Thursday to Monday—and he's not going back on his word."

"Did you get it in writing?" Ivy was joking. Sort of.

"Without me, there's no movie," Jacey reminded them. "And I don't think we need reshoots, anyway. Not the ones Adam wants."

In preparation for the shop op, ever practical Ivy had suggested calling a few stores ahead of time, asking them to close so Jacey could peruse the racks without distraction.

"No way," Jacey had said dismissively. "That's too obnoxious."

"If you say so. But it's the only way you're gonna be able to seriously shop without fans or press on your trunk," her cousin reasoned.

"Oh, come on, it's not like I'm Oprah, Uma, or Madonna! Besides, it'll make me look even worse if the press gets hold of it. Julia Barton doesn't make the stores close for her. Why should I?"

"Because," Dash said, "right now, you're a bigger story than she is. If you're serious about getting a prom dress, we need to be discreet, fly under the radar."

She'd stood her ground. "I will not ask Ron Herman or Fred Segal or Max Azria to close up shop for me. That's taking the star thing too far."

Ivy pulled up to their first stop. Fred Segal, a hip and funky designer store, was set up as a series of small boutiques, featuring cutting-edge clothes, shoes, cosmetics, jewelry, gifts, books, greeting cards—pretty much everything—under one roof. Jacey forgot about Adam and *Galaxy* instantly.

She dangled a stained-glass and Swarovski crystal pendant. "How fabulous is this?" she asked excitedly.

It was too easy to get distracted from her prom-dress mission, especially when a salesperson, recognizing her, offered to trail behind and carry her selections. On the way to the designer dresses, Jacey just pointed at merchandise and those items got added to her stash. She passed a selection of cashmere sweaters and had to pick up a blue wrap for her mom. Wandering through the menswear department, she found a down vest for her stepdad—and, oh! "We need jeans!" she called out.

All three girls ended up with several pairs of Rebel Yell, True Religion, AG, and vintage, left-weave Levis. For Logan, she bought a $250 pair of Tommy Hilfiger jeans. Then she found an awesome sweater to go with them.

She'd told her crew anything they wanted was on her tab.

"It's like supermarket sweepstakes—grab and run!" giggled a delighted Desi.

When they reached the dresses, Jacey quickly decided that none were right for the prom.

"Okay, we have to hit Kitson's," Ivy said. "It's by far the coolest place you have ever seen. The dresses totally rock."

Kitson's had made a name for itself selling one-of-a-kind merchandise by hot new designers, including exclusive stuff by Gwen Stefani and Justin Timberlake. It featured everything from clothes—cute T-shirts and trousers, jeans, tops, skirts, dresses—to sneakers, accessories, and gifts galore.

An even more serious buying spree ensued. Jacey picked up baby stuff worthy of Suri Cruise and Shiloh Jolie-Pitt. Sartorially, those celebri-tots would have nothing on her baby brother!

As if on cue, Desi suddenly held up a teeny pink

T-shirt, loudly demanding, "What size is this? Fetus?"

Everyone laughed, which was unfortunate, in that it called attention to Jacey. Word quickly spread that Jacey Chandliss and her posse were shopping. Fans rushed at her.

All four feet eleven inches of Desi guarded her protectively. Ivy summoned the store manager, who informed them that if they didn't want the attention, they ought to have called ahead—the store would have gladly shut its doors for them.

So they called ahead to Ron Herman, an excellent boutique that carried the hippest new designers and trends. If Jacey was going to make a statement at the prom, she'd find the punctuation here. The staff at the store put a "Closed—Private Sale" sign in the window and ushered them in.

The dresses lived up to the advertising. As Jacey moved through rack upon rack of killer outfits, she began to mellow out, even to think more kindly about her current film. Was it possible *Galaxy Rangers* wasn't as craptastic as she thought? She mentally reviewed the day's shooting.

Nah. It sucked the big one.

Irony alert. If she'd stayed home, she'd have been starring in the school play as Elphaba, the misunderstood witch in *Wicked*. A classic play, a challenging character, altogether more soul-satisfying than the cartoonish character of Zorina!

If she'd stayed home, she'd have been with Logan right this minute.

If she'd stayed home—

"Jacey, you *have* to see this dress. This dress is so you. It's like it was made for you." Ivy was holding a bold red silk-and-chiffon, single-shoulder-strap, baby-doll dress by Marni.

"Excellent choice! This is vintage, so fresh and new!" The salesperson beamed, dopily contradicting herself.

"It's over two thousand dollars. Is that 'cause it's old *and* new?" Desi asked.

"Who cares? No one in Bloomfield Hills will be wearing this!" Jacey exclaimed, trying it on. Ivy had guessed correctly: it did look amazing on her.

"Your phone's been vibrating nonstop since we got here," Desi pointed out. "Want me to get it?"

Jacey's phone dangled from her Balenciaga bag. She made no moves to answer it.

"What if it's an emergency? What if it's Dash? Or Logan? Or . . . Matt?" Desi teased. "Or all three? 'Cause whoever's trying to get you isn't giving up." The phone kept buzzing.

"All three can wait," Jacey joyfully rejoined. "My prom dress? Shoes? Earrings? They cannot wait. And . . . omigod, I forgot about my hair! Has anyone called my hairdresser? Can I fly him to Michigan?" She looked around for Ivy—who happened to be striding her way, cell phone nestled between her shoulder and ear, arms filled with clothes, promising whoever was on the other end, "Okay, okay, I'll put her on."

The look on Ivy's face said it all: "You so do not want to take this call."

Jacey Demands Stores
Close Doors for Her!

What's a baby diva to do when she craves a shop op at L.A.'s trendiest place? And she doesn't—repeat, DOES NOT—want to be disturbed? Does she tuck those golden-red waves 'neath a baseball cap, hide those anime eyes behind big, dark sunglasses? Or . . . uh . . . let's see, maybe venture out *without* an attention-grabbing entourage? Nah. So much easier to demand that hip boutiques lock out the public, so Ms. Chandliss may scope without those bothersome fans and photogs who made her famous in the first place. Way to curry favor with your public, Jace—wonder who'd vote for you now!

Chapter Twelve

Okay, Officially Miserable Now

"You have to fix this!" Jacey wailed. They were still at Ron Herman. She was on the phone with Cinnamon, well into a righteous hissy fit. "They *promised* me the time off!"

"They insist on the reshoots this weekend," Cinnamon repeated sympathetically. "There's no other time they can do them, and they need you."

While Jacey and her friends had been blithely buying up half of Melrose Avenue, the *Galaxy Rangers* honchos had apparently made an executive—and nonnegotiable—decision. They'd rewritten her scenes.

"In the last few hours, the script changed? How is that possible?" Jacey was incensed.

Adam-the-Screen-Hog Pratt had somehow convinced

Emory, and the producers, that *his* character was too dim-witted, *hers* was too smart, and a love scene between them would go a long way toward fixing what ailed *Galaxy Rangers*.

A love scene with Adam? Jacey put her finger to her temple as if to say, "Shoot me now." She wasn't even going there. Miss the prom? Logan had asked her with roses. She'd said yes with tears. Their big night to reconnect was five days away!

Cinnamon had to derail the evil Emory-Adam axis—it was imperative!

Her agent balked at Jacey's demand. "I don't have that kind of power."

"This is crazy!" Jacey argued. "The movie needs changes, but not the ones they're talking about. *And* they *know* I'm out of town this weekend!"

"With all due respect, my young client, this is only your second movie, and last time I checked, you weren't a screenwriter. Can you really say these changes are bad?" Cinnamon challenged her.

She clenched her jaw. "This is all about Adam getting a bigger part! I don't have to be a screenwriter to know when someone's using me. All this happened after *Four Sisters* came out. I'm a star now. He's being so obvious!" Jacey was so frustrated she almost went all Naomi

Campbell and flung the phone across the room.

Cinnamon calmly reiterated what she had been told: Jacey was needed on the set every day that week, including Friday, Saturday, and Sunday.

"No." Jacey pressed her lips together.

"No?" Cinnamon sounded surprised—and not in a good way. "Jacey, you have neither the right nor the power to say no. I'm sorry."

Sorry won't cut it, thought Jacey. She didn't care whether she had the power or not. Thursday night, she would be on a plane to Michigan. Monday morning, she'd be back on the *Galaxy Rangers* set. In between, she'd be with her family and her boyfriend. Kickin' butt, as his date, at his prom. As planned. As *promised*.

There was either a long sigh on the other end of the phone, or Jacey had driven Cinnamon to smoking. Finally, the agent said, "Put Ivy on."

Ivy took the call in a private room at the back of the store. While they worked it out—Jacey was sure they would, they always came through for her—she forged ahead and put the red dress on her charge card. The salesperson brought over a selection of shoes. Desi helped her choose a black patent-leather pair with red soles and lent Jacey her phone, so she could call her favorite hairdresser, Yuki of Beverly Hills. She hadn't finished dialing, when Ivy returned, plucked the phone from her hand, and folded it shut. "Listen, cuz, let's not freak out," Ivy was trying to remain upbeat. "We'll figure a way out of this mess. I convinced Cinnamon to dig, find out what the big emergency really is. Maybe you won't have to cancel the prom."

"No maybes about it," Jacey groused. "Nothing's getting canceled."

The interview with *US Weekly* was the last thing Jacey wanted to do that afternoon. But it'd been promised, and Jacey refused to be like some other people in Hollywood and welsh on promises.

Peyton was waiting for them at an outdoor table at The Ivy, a pricey celebri-lunch haunt which, coincidentally, had the same name as Jacey's cousin. It had been chosen to impress the reporter, as well as various random photographers who were always planted outside.

The deal was that *US Weekly* got an exclusive with Jacey, in exchange for a puff piece, an article meant to defuse the "ridiculously-blown-out-of-proportion rumors" about exactly what had happened at her house when the cops came.

Jacey wasn't to be defensive. She was to laugh at the way things had gotten out of hand, and to set the record straight. She was to explain that, really, the worst thing that had happened at the pool party was people getting splashed, and, possibly, the music had been too loud.

The reporter dutifully wrote everything down in his notebook. "Good clean fun," he mused.

"Exactly," Peyton said, moving the interview along.

Jacey was distracted and irritated, worrying about the prom and Logan. Suddenly, everything Desi did annoyed her, such as constantly looking around to see if any stars were there; clutching her cell-phone camera just in case; and ranting loudly about the prices. ("Oh, my God! They charge $23.50 for a bowl of vegetable soup! What's in it, golden potatoes with real gold?")

The reporter turned his attention to her loud friend. "You were involved in the car crash, right? What can you tell us about the accident? Were you drinking? I hear you totaled the car."

"No way!" Desi bellowed.

"How did you lose control of the wheel, then? You went right up on the sidewalk, into a city park, and slammed into a statue."

"We're paying for the damage," Peyton interjected.

All along, Desi insisted she hadn't lost control. Jacey thought differently. That car was lightning-fast. The slightest touch on the gas pedal would send it shooting down the road. Desi had anything but a light touch. The section of Sunset Boulevard where the accident had happened was very winding. Jacey could guess what'd probably happened. So when Desi lied, and blurted out that the paparazzi had run her off the road, Jacey's jaw dropped, and Peyton ended the interview abruptly.

At just past seven in the evening, Jacey, Dash, Desi, and Ivy gathered in the spa bathroom, listening to Cinnamon on speakerphone delivering the news on the new wrinkle in the *Galaxy Rangers* filming situation. Jacey sprawled out in the empty Jacuzzi, arms and legs flopping over the sides; Desi had parked herself next to Dash on the marble floor by the fireplace; Ivy was perched on the vanity.

"So, what you're saying," Ivy said, evidently finding it hard to believe, "is that it all started with Adam?"

"I knew it!" shouted Jacey. "That's what makes it such a joke!"

"Adam apparently came up with good suggestions, at least that's the story they're sticking to. Emory agreed, they took it to the producers, and—"

"How does Adam get that much clout?" Dash butted in. "He's a nobody."

The sound on the other end of the speakerphone was probably Cinnamon taking a long drag on a cigarette. "As I was saying, the changes were approved by the studio head. That's as high as it goes, girls and boy. There's nothing we can do."

"There has to be!" Desi cried. "It's her prom."

There was silence on the other end of the phone.

"We know it may sound juvenile," Dash pleaded, "but this is a big part of Jacey's life, and they can't *want* to make her unhappy."

"It's gone beyond what she wants," Cinnamon informed them. "Jacey signed a contract. They're expecting her to live up to it, to be professional."

"I am!" Jacey exploded, "I'm the one who's doing everything I'm supposed to. I asked nicely for the time off. A deal's a deal, and I am totally holding up my end."

"I'm really sorry, Jacey. I know this weekend meant a lot to you. But you have to cancel the trip."

"What if we make it seem like she's doing them a favor?" Ivy—who'd taken a few pages from Peyton's spin book—suggested. "Tell them that even though Jacey disagrees with the changes, she'll do them—any other weekend."

"Believe me, I tried that," Cinnamon said wearily. "I went over the schedule *personally*. They can't add days on to the schedule."

"Why not?" Desi asked.

"Other people have commitments beyond the shoot dates," Cinnamon explained. "They won't be available."

"What about me?" Jacey demanded. "What about my commitment this weekend? How come my time isn't as important as everyone else's?" A lump in her throat formed. "What if," Jacey said desperately, "I never got this message? What if I just don't show up on Friday? Or pretend to be dehydrated and exhausted in the hospital?"

"Don't even think about it!" her agent barked. Suddenly, there was a different Cinnamon on the phone, one who'd run out of patience and declarations of "fabulous!" "You can't be paid like a professional and then act like a child. If you don't show up, your reputation *will* suffer."

With epic bad timing, Desi made a joke. "If she plays hooky, it'll be on her permanent record?"

"What don't you get about this?" Cinnamon growled. "They could sue her—ask for every dime back—and more. In this business, one selfish decision affects lots of other people, including the salaries of everyone working on the movie—which are nowhere near yours, I assure you. You have to make sacrifices, do things you don't want to. That's what it means to grow up."

"With great power, with great big bucks, comes great responsibility," Dash said, trying for levity, but misquoting Spider-Man.

They heard Cinnamon sigh on the other end of the phone. "It's out of my hands, Jacey. No matter how it happened, whether it was Adam, or Emory realizing changes were needed, the studio agreed. You have to cancel your weekend plans and be there."

"That's not fair!" Jacey kicked the side of her $20,000 Jacuzzi with her $350 sandals.

The room went silent, because each and every one of them—Jacey included—knew exactly what Cinnamon was going to say.

"Do. Not. Go. There. Jacey. Do not talk about fair, unless you're prepared to give up everything good that's been given to you. I am not saying you didn't earn it. But really, is it fair that people go hungry every day and you're spending money on everything you see? Don't make me the bad guy here. Just show up on the set with your new lines memorized, and be grateful for this opportunity." Cinnamon hung up, not waiting for a reply.

Good! Jacey didn't want to hear her anymore. She wanted to blame her. "I bet Cinnamon's not fighting for me at all. She's got a major stake in this—like fifteen percent!"

"Whoa," Dash held up his palm. "This is not her fault."

"She's siding with them," Jacey pouted. "Otherwise, she could fix this."

"You're being ridiculous," Desi argued.

"I'll quit. I'll just quit. I'll go home. This movie is so lame anyway. It's not worth losing my boyfriend over." Jacey didn't even realize she was crying. She barely heard her cousin Ivy whisper, "If he's really the one, he'll understand."

"How am I gonna tell him?" Jacey whimpered, tears streaming down her face. "Give me a script for that." She bounded up to her rooftop terrace and plopped into a recliner. There *had* to be a way to get home for the prom without torpedoing her career. She watched the palm trees around her swaying like a metronome. *Stay. Go. Go. Stay.* They echoed the rhythm of her thoughts.

Go home to Logan. Be prom queen to his prom king. Get in major trouble with Cinnamon.

Stay here, honor my commitment. Break Logan's heart.

Go home, spend time with Mom. Get blamed for screwing up Galaxy Rangers. *Bankrupt the crew.*

Stay here, accept responsibility. Grow up. Lose my boyfriend.

Jacey paced up and down on the terrace.

What would movie characters do? In the *Little Women*-based *Four Sisters*, strong, rebellious Jo would go to Logan, consequences be damned. And righteous Meg? Totally stay here, do the job contracted for. Selfish Amy? Go, because she'd be prom queen! And boring old Beth? Die, probably.

No matter what fictional character she chose, whether

Catherine and Heathcliff from *Wuthering Heights*, Romeo and Juliet, or even Meredith and McDreamy from *Grey's Anatomy*, she couldn't summon up a helpful scenario.

She summoned the next best thing.

"Mom?" It was late back east, but Jacey's mom was a night owl.

"What's wrong?" asked Cece, instantly anxious.

"Nothing," Jacey assured her. "We're all fine. It's just . . . I need advice."

Jacey's mom listened to her daughter's tale of woe.

The presence of a sympathetic voice on the other end of the phone, someone who loved her unconditionally, who didn't want anything from her, allowed Jacey to voice feelings she didn't even know she had. "I don't want to do this stupid movie. I want to come home."

"Are you sure that's what this is about?"

Jacey was surprised by her mom's response. "What do you mean?"

"Ouch!" her mom suddenly giggled. "Sorry, that brother of yours has strong legs—or elbows, or whatever he's pummeling me with."

Jacey blew her nose. "He's kicking already? You didn't tell me that!"

"Just started. Anyway, sweetie, let's get back to your problem."

"What should I do, Mom? There's so much pressure! They're laying this guilt trip on me, that I'll, like, bankrupt all the crew members or something."

"That sounds like an exaggeration, but let's root out what's upsetting you so much." Cece's voice was assured, soothing. "Why do you really want to blow off the movie and come home? Is it the prom itself?"

Well, yeah! Jacey had totally pictured arriving at the dance in that awesome dress, a hometown heroine, sprinkled with fairy dust, the envy of the senior class; the prom queen, on the arm of the to-die-for prom king.

"Maybe this will help," Cece suggested. "What if I was having the baby the same night as the prom. Where would you choose to be?"

"No choice! Of *course* I'd be with you."

"Okay," her mom said carefully, "maybe it's not the dance itself that's pulling you. Is it Logan?"

That was more complicated, and her mom knew it.

"Is it that you can't stand another day without him, or you can't stomach the idea of disappointing him?"

"He'll be crushed, Mom."

"Him, or his ego? Because his ego is resilient. It will rebound."

Jacey swallowed. "I don't want to hurt him."

"Of course you don't! Logan's your boyfriend. You'd do

anything possible not to hurt him. Only not everything is in your power."

"What if he breaks up with me, Mom?" Jacey whispered.

Her mom remained silent.

"I'll be crushed."

Jacey, or her ego? Her mom didn't have to say it. Cece continued, "Try this. If the movie you were doing was one you loved, say, *Four Sisters*; if Julia Barton requested changes, not Adam Pratt; if you were asked to film extra sequences in that scenario. Would you be this conflicted?"

"Was that a rhetorical question?" Jacey mumbled, knowing that while it'd kill her, she'd still choose the movie over the prom.

"Here's what I know," Cece said softly. "From the time you could talk, you could act. From the moment you saw your first TV show, your first movie, you wanted to be an actress. That's been your only dream. Then *Generation Next* came along and gave you a shot."

"I know, and I'm grateful," Jacey admitted.

"This summer is a reality check," Cece went on, "allowing you to live your dream. Maybe you'll find out you're not ready to go pro. That's all right. You can always come home. On the other hand, this summer's experiences could just as easily validate what you always thought—acting *is* your passion. Even bad choices of movies can teach you something."

"You know what's so bogus?" Jacey moaned. "In all the movies, all the inspirational books and stuff, when you have a choice to make, they always say, 'Follow your heart.' What if your heart is in more than one place? With acting, and with Logan? With Hollywood and with home? Why can't it be in both places?"

"It can, Jacey. You just can't *have* both. Not this time."

Jacey paced the patio long after she'd said good night to her mom. What if . . . ?

An idea dawned. No one had suggested a compromise—filming for most of the weekend, but squeezing in just enough of a break to make it to the prom. Was it too complicated to work?

Jacey dashed to her bedroom, grabbed a pen and paper, and mapped out the timing.

"That's awesome!" ever loyal Desi exclaimed when Jacey presented the potential plan to her friends. "Genius!"

"It'll depend on compromises," Jacey warned. "Lots o' compromises."

"Not to mention money!" Dash declared. "Can you even fathom what a private plane costs?"

"So let's *not* mention money!" Jacey jested. "But while

you're calculating, don't forget, we'll need a pilot. And I think they insist on a flight attendant, too." Jacey ticked off other some requirements: hairdresser, makeup artist, manicurist, and a down-to-the-split-second schedule everyone would have to follow.

"What if you get delayed?" Ivy fretted. "Happens all the time—due to storms, all kinds of weather conditions. You can't pay off Mother Nature. Then you'll have promised Logan something you ultimately can't deliver. This is dicey, Jace."

Jacey eyed her cousin. "Are ya feeling lucky? 'Cause I am."

Logan, as it turned out, wasn't so much feeling the luck—or the love, for that matter. Bummed at Jacey's change of plans, he didn't understand why his girlfriend would have to miss all the preprom festivities, or the post-prom breakfast on Sunday. "You said they promised you the time off," he repeated.

"All of Saturday night is ours," Jacey reminded him, remaining positive. "The prom. And after the prom. I'll be there for the best part. I promise!"

A Diva's Dilemma

Whispers of trouble on the *Galaxy Rangers* set have officially turned into a shouting match, with our girl Jacey loudest of all! Sources say she despises the script so much she's actually telling people it's gonna go straight to video! Does she think going all insubordinate on director Emory Farber's ass will help? Could it be she and Adam Pratt had a falling out?

Put yourself in poor Adam's shoes. The newcomer is simply doing his best to save the movie—while diva-doll Jacey (who led him on?) uses her clout to sink it. What gives, Jacey? We'd think she'd be doing everything she could to help, not hurt *Galaxy Rangers*.

We sent you to Hollywood to make us proud, not get all demanding, nasty, and loud! Here's a thought: could she be learning the art of contrary from her NBF, Matt Canseco? Sources say that unbeknownst to the boy back home, Logan, and to the detriment of Adam, these two are in constant touch.

Chapter Thirteen

. . . And We're Off!

If only her friends could figure out how to squash that
blog! Alas, they were busy doing other things. The rest of
that week they dedicated 24-7 to making Jacey's compromise plan a reality. Dash worked on securing a private jet.
It would then have to be on the runway, ready to take off
on a moment's notice. It would then have to sit at the
small Wayne County airport outside Detroit for eighteen
hours, ready to wing Jacey back to L.A. in time for
Sunday's shoot. A licensed pilot and flight attendant had
to be hired for the same time period.

Yuki, Jacey's hairdresser, refused to travel to "that fly-
over state" without an entourage. Ivy bargained him down
to one assistant, one "shampoo girl," and a photographer

—to document the in-flight experience for his hoped-for reality show, *Hair, There & Everywhere.*

Ivy agreed to pay time and a half for a makeup artist. "She's supposed to be the best."

"What about the manicurist?" Jacey asked.

"We'll get right on it. You don't need a separate pedicurist, Princess-of-the-Prom, do you?" Ivy quipped.

It would be Desi's job to make sure Jacey's red dress and her shoes, bag, jewelry, and accessories were on the plane. It was Dash, of course, who remembered that they needed a boutonniere for Logan's lapel. He chose a white calla lily.

The biggest tasks were left for Jacey herself: convincing Emory to let her have Saturday off, and getting Adam on her side. Jacey considered what she'd learned about Hollywood. The town operated on a quid pro quo basis— "You give me what I want, I'll give you what you want."

Adam wanted publicity. He agreed to work on Jacey's scenes all day Friday, and Saturday morning, allowing her to leave by noon. In exchange, Jacey promised to do an interview in a major magazine with him. She agreed to say what a fabulous new talent had been found in Adam Pratt, how much she adored working with him.

Emory was more of a puzzle. *Galaxy Rangers* was his first big picture, and he didn't want to screw it up. He wanted the film to be a success: in other words, he needed a miracle.

Jacey could help by endorsing it. She could allow a TV reporter to interview her at the prom, where she'd say how great *Galaxy Rangers* was going to be.

Emory went for it.

Although Cinnamon balked, and Peyton worried about backlash, Jacey got her way. All day Thursday and Friday, thoughts of the prom and Logan danced in her head while she recited her new lines, kissed Adam—that is, Zartagnan—and did whatever the new scenes called for, quickly and efficiently. The crew called her One-Take Jacey.

"When you're really motivated," noted an impressed Emory after the first scene on Saturday morning, "you can be amazing, Jacey. I know you want to get out of here quickly, but I hope this also means you believe in the new scenes."

A wave of guilt and shame washed over her. The young director's fear of failure had blinded him. She cast her eyes at the clock on the wall. It was 9:17 a.m. In less than three hours, she'd be airborne.

At the break, Jacey retreated to her trailer and called her friends. "We're on schedule. Will the car be ready by noon?"

Dash promised it would; Desi assured her the outfits were already on board. Ivy would personally escort Yuki and the team to the airstrip in plenty of time. Jacey then called Logan, who was on his way to one of several pre-prom events. She told him she'd be there by eight that evening, "if not sooner." She neglected to mention the part about the reporter covering the first part of the night. She hoped Logan wouldn't mind. She hoped that the sight of her, in that dress, would captivate him and take his mind off everything else.

At eleven in the morning, with one hour to go, the AD knocked on her trailer door with a newsflash: Emory had taken a quick look at the rushes—unedited footage of the scenes they'd just shot—and realized Zartagnan was in the wrong outfit. It didn't match the one he had worn in the previous scene.

They needed a reshoot.

"How come no one noticed this before?" Jacey blasted him. "Don't you pay someone to check for continuity?"

That person wasn't on the set today.

"Wrong answer!" Jacey growled. "And what about you?" She turned to face a chagrined Adam. "How could you not know you're in the wrong stupid outfit?"

"You didn't notice it, either, Jacey," Adam pointed out.

Emory appeared and put his arm around her shoulders.

"Calm down. We'll get it done quickly. You'll be out of here by one p.m. Okay?"

Jacey softened. Emory was not the brightest light on the Christmas tree—he was misguided, tentative, and frightened of failure—but he had empathy for her and for her situation. He was being nice.

And, as it turned out, true to his word.

"An hour off schedule, that's not so bad," Dash reassured her, as Jacey ducked into the revved-up Ford Explorer.

A half hour later, they pulled up at the runway, next to the leased Gulfstream jet.

"Good luck." Dash gave Jacey a kiss.

"See you tomorrow, prom queen," Desi added. "Take pictures."

She hugged them both. "I love you guys; you know that, right?"

Ivy, the only posse member set to accompany her to Michigan, was waiting in the plane's plush cabin, along with Yuki and his entourage, plus makeup artist Erbe, manicurist Kim, and an intrusive photographer, who snapped Jacey's every move.

She didn't care. She was focused on getting off the ground, getting home.

"Let the transformation begin!" declared Yuki as soon as

they reached cruising altitude. His shampoo girl escorted Jacey to the deluxe bathroom aboard the craft to scrub all traces of Zorina's spikes out of her hair and get it conditioned and ready for Yuki.

Erbe used some gentle skin cleanser to remove the heavy makeup; Kim went to work on the space-girl nail polish. At one point, Jacey, stretched out on a lounge seat, had three people working on her at once: hairdresser, manicurist, and makeup artist.

"How does it feel being waited on hand and foot—literally—at thirty thousand miles in the air?" Ivy asked with a chuckle.

"It would be awesome, if I weren't such a nervous wreck!" Jacey admitted. "How're we doing on time?"

"Cuz, relax. It's gonna be all right. You want a drink?"

"No way," Jacey pointed to her stomach. "I would so not hold anything down right now."

As soon as her manicure dried, Jacey called her mom from the plane. If there were no delays, perhaps Cece could ride over in the limo from the airport to the prom with her. That was the only way they'd get some face (and tummy) time, in. How cool would it be if Jacey could feel the baby kick?

Her mom agreed, but insisted Jacey not sweat it. "Just be safe," Cece said, "and don't overdo it."

Yuki spent hours on Jacey's hair—partly because he wanted the photographer to get him blow-drying and styling from all angles, and partly because Jacey suddenly decided she "needed" highlights. Luckily, Yuki's assistant had brought along all possible combinations of colors.

With under two hours left on the four-hour flight, Jacey slipped on the dress: it had been altered to perfection, cinched to show off her small waist; the one-shoulder strap was alluring. The flowy skirt made her feel like dancing already!

She was about to slip into her so-five-minutes-from-now Christian Louboutin slingbacks when she realized she'd forgotten to bring pantyhose. What were the chances, she mused, searching through the luggage, that Desi had remembered?

"Guess you'll have to do without," Ivy said. "Can you manage?"

"No. Can you call Victoria's Secret, tell them it's for me, and we'll pay to have them delivered to the plane when we land?"

"You're kidding, right?" Ivy's jaw dropped.

"I just want everything to be perfect. And we can afford it, can't we?"

"I guess," Ivy said tentatively. "You don't think that's a little . . . extreme?"

"More extreme than all this?" Jacey gestured at the private plane-slash-dressing room.

Finally, with a half hour to go, Jacey was dressed, made up, manicured, pedicured, highlighted, and updo'd. She looked killer, if she did say so herself!

The pilot's voice came over the loudspeaker. "Air traffic control is slowing us down. There's a delay in the Detroit area; we'll have to circle."

"No way!" Jacey jumped up and started to head toward the cockpit, nearly slipping in her new shoes. "We have no time to circle! I have a prom!"

Chapter Fourteen

Starry, Starry Night

Logan met her under the portico of the entrance to the Marriott Hotel, where the prom was being held. The theme was "Starry, Starry Night," and the sight of Logan in a midnight blue tux practically took her breath away.

Her tall, blond, buff boyfriend enveloped her in his arms, and pressed her so close to him she heard his heart beating wildly.

"Jacey," he murmured, "I thought you weren't going to make it. I was so nervous."

"There were all these delays. I'm sorry, I couldn't help it."

"Jace?" Logan pulled away a bit. "It wasn't cool to call

them up and ask them to start the prom later. No one appreciated it."

She batted her eyelashes. "I just wanted to spend the entire prom with you. I didn't want to miss a single minute."

He exhaled, looked into her eyes. "I know. And, uh, Jace? There's a reporter waiting over there; says you promised him an interview. That's not true, right?"

"I kinda had to—just one of the many hoops I had to jump through to get here."

Logan had gotten a haircut since she had last seen him. He looked so clean, so freshly shaven, so salt of the Midwestern earth—and now, so borderline annoyed. "You're kidding, right?"

"I'll get rid of him quickly," Jacey promised. "I really missed you, Logan."

"I missed you too, Jacey."

"Show me how much." Jacey tipped her head up, stood on her toes, and moved to kiss him.

He stopped her. "Not now. You're really late. We should get inside. "Here—" the corsage he'd bought was in its container, resting on a ledge. It was a minibouquet of the same pink roses he'd sent to L.A. Logan's hands trembled as he started to pin it on her.

Jacey's heart sank. The flowers were pink. Her dress

was red. It would clash, but she didn't want to hurt Logan's feelings by not wearing it.

He put it on her.

Jacey produced the boutonniere, pinned it on him, and silently thanked Dash for remembering. Logan took her arm and guided her inside, down the hotel hallway, and toward the ballroom.

He'll tell me how amazing I look once we get inside and there's actual light, Jacey thought.

Perhaps he might have, but as soon as they made their way inside the ballroom, the reporter was in Jacey's face, which led to a crowd running up to welcome her and gush over her dress, her shoes, her bag, and her jewelry.

Some promgoers were not cheering. Above the fandemonium, Jacey heard the snide comments of the girls who dissed her.

"Oooh, look at Miss Thing, the Hollywood diva."

"A real-life starlet in our humble school."

Jacey asked the reporter if he would mind giving her an hour. Surely he could understand that she wanted to greet her friends, apologize for arriving so late, and dance with Logan. The reporter grudgingly agreed. "Half hour, it's Saturday night, and you're not the only one with plans."

"I know. I'm sure you didn't intend spending yours at

a high school prom. Don't worry—I'll give good sound bite, I promise." Jacey shot him a megawatt smile and sauntered away.

Logan led Jacey over to the bar. "Your usual? Diet Coke?"

"I kind of stopped drinking pop," Jacey admitted. "In L.A., everyone drinks water. Do they have sparkling?"

"Club soda," the bartender—who was also Logan's history teacher, Mr. Jonas—offered. "Best we can do."

"That's great," Jacey said, deciding against asking for a lime wedge. The ballroom had been decorated in shades of blue and silver. Crinkly silver stars twinkled from the ceiling, and bouquets of blue and silver balloons served as centerpieces.

"So what do you think? We did some kick-ass job, huh?" The blond, fake-baked Tiffany West was suddenly at the bar, standing next to them. "I even got Logan to pitch in," she said with a wink.

"It looks . . . super." Jacey tried to sound sincere, but her acting skills failed her. It was at that moment that she realized what Tiffany had gotten for graduation: new boobs. The girl was proudly displaying them in a deep V-necked wrap dress.

"Too bad you got here so late," Tiffany said when Logan turned away from them. "They already did the ballots for prom king and queen."

"Well, I'm sure my boyfriend got enough votes without mine," Jacey slipped a proprietary arm around Logan's waist.

"Yo, my man!" Three of Logan's basketball teammates and their dates made their way over, which Logan seemed relieved about. Jacey knew two of them vaguely and wanted to find out what colleges they were going to in the fall, but their dates were all over her.

"Where'd you get that dress?"

"How much were the shoes?"

"Where can I buy that bag?"

She wanted Logan to rescue her, and to ask her to dance. She got half her wish: she was extracted from the circle of admirers, only not by Logan. The reporter, tapping his watch, shoved a mic in her face.

Jacey led him over to a corner of the room, and, as promised, talked a great game about *Galaxy Rangers*, stressing the fact that Emory Farber was the next big director on the scene and that everyone should circle the film's release date on their calendar.

A couple of behind-the-scenes sound bites later, Jacey was satisfied that she'd kept her promise, and thanked the reporter. When she returned to the dance floor, she spied Logan, surrounded by a bunch of his classmates, including

Tiffany and Beth; they were drinking, laughing, and seemingly having a great time. Jacey made her way over to him.

"Let's dance," she said, just as the band kicked in.

Jacey couldn't help noticing the sea of blue dresses, including Tiffany's, on the dance floor. She felt very . . . red.

Finally, a slow dance came on, and Jacey was grateful for it. She rested her head against Logan's chest and reached her arms around his neck, as he pulled her close. Jacey thought of a scene from the classic movie musical *West Side Story*, one of her grandmother's favorites. It was the dance scene, when star-crossed lovers Tony and Maria were in a ballroom full of people, and slowly, everyone faded away, because the two saw only each other. "That's true love," her grandmother would say with a sigh.

Jacey so wanted to feel that way. She didn't. Maybe because they kept being interrupted every two seconds! Dancers leaned over to introduce themselves to Jacey and give Logan the thumbs-up for having the most famous prom date in the history of Bloomfield High.

All the accolades and comments made Jacey feel less like Logan's girlfriend and more like his trophy date.

The band switched to a mix of dance, hip-hop, and rock tunes. The dance floor was packed with gyrating promgoers.

And then, jarringly, the music was suddenly silenced: Principal Pell's voice boomed out of a microphone at the front of the ballroom. "Attention, everyone! We've come to the most highly anticipated moment of the night. We're ready to announce who you chose to be your prom king and prom queen."

There was an excited tittering, and then a hush fell over the crowd as the principal held up a sheet of paper. "Without further ado," she said, "the graduating class of Bloomfield Hills High School, your prom king is . . . Logan Finnerty!"

The ballroom erupted in wild applause. Jacey joined in delightedly, planting a huge kiss on her boyfriend's lips. Logan smooched the top of her head and made his way up to the stage.

"And your prom queen is . . ."

Jacey cast her gaze downward and crossed her fingers behind her back. There was no way she could expect it to be her; as Tiffany pointed out, her tardiness made her ineligible. Only, just then . . . how perfect would it be if Principal Pell announced *her* name?

"Tiffany West!"

Jacey watched Logan and Tiffany dance to the official prom song, "You're Beautiful." It'd been one of her favorite romantic songs. Until now. She caught Logan closing his eyes briefly as he danced with Tiff—did he close his eyes dreamily when he danced with Jacey?

When the song ended, the dance floor again erupted in cheers, and people went up to congratulate Logan and Tiffany. Eventually, he made his way back to Jacey's side.

"Wow—can't pretend I wasn't expecting this, but it's a rush." Logan was beaming, his eyes sparkling.

"I'm sorry I was ineligible. I thought I had a shot at being queen, but I couldn't help arriving late."

"You weren't ineligible," Logan said. "I think . . . well, I guess Tiff just got a few more votes." He tried to make light of it, seeing her face fall. "Anyway, it's just a high school dance."

"Yeah, just a dance." One that she'd spent thousands on, lied for, and possibly compromised her career to be at.

The prom ended just after midnight. Jacey had assumed Logan had booked a room at the hotel. Wasn't that what you did, the night of the prom? Especially when you'd been together two years and hadn't gone all the way yet?

However, Logan had not booked a room. He'd made other plans entirely. "We've got three parties to go to," he told her. "I planned on spending quality time alone with you tomorrow."

"But I'm not staying until tomorrow," Jacey said.

"But I didn't know that when I told all the guys I'd be there." She could tell by his face that it didn't matter how she looked, what a big star she was—or that she still wanted him to be her first. Logan was going to party all night long.

"You didn't tell me you wanted to spend the whole night hanging with, like, a million people," she said, trying to keep the disappointment out of her voice.

"A million people I might never see again," he pointed out. "In September, everyone goes their separate ways. We won't all be together again—ever."

"Logan," Jacey said once they were in the car, "do you have any idea what it took for me to get here?"

"A lot?" Stopping for a light, he turned to her, and gave her a cute look.

She sighed. If she'd known her entire eighteen hours were going to be spent among a bunch of drunken, partying high school seniors, she might not have come.

"Maybe we could sneak off," she suggested, "after a few hours?"

"Maybe!" he agreed. Then he leaned over and kissed her. Lightly, sweetly.

Maybe this will get him to change his mind about all the party-hopping, she thought, leaning into him. She put her arms around his neck, pulled him close, and kissed him hard and passionately.

Logan returned her intensity, and they kissed long after the light had turned green. Cars behind them started honking, and they broke away from each other at last.

Logan smiled and winked at her.

Jacey stared straight ahead. It was the first time she'd ever kissed Logan and felt . . . nothing.

By four in the morning, at the last party, in Tiffany's house, she was half-asleep. Jacey left Logan there when the limo arrived to take her to the plane.

Sunday was one *lo-o-o-ong* day—an extra three hours long, courtesy of three times zones, flying east to west. Jacey spent most of it sleepwalking through her scenes on the *Galaxy* set. Which made no one happy, least of all Emory and Adam. They hadn't tweaked the schedule just so she could ruin Sunday's shoot because of exhaustion.

Too tired to contradict them, Jacey apologized, promising to do better on Monday.

When the limo delivered her home, she found her grand mansion very quiet. No one was around. Jacey plopped on the couch and switched on the TV. She flipped open her cell phone to listen to her messages. Dash, Aja,

Ivy, and Emilio were going to Dolce, the restaurant co-owned by Ashton Kutcher, for dinner. After that, they were going to Mood. She was welcome to join them wherever. Dash added that if she didn't want to go out, but wanted company, he'd come home.

Jacey smiled. God, how she loved Dash. He was the most unselfish, thoughtful guy on the planet. She hoped Aja was deserving.

Desi had left a text message. She was going out with "a couple people." Curiously, she didn't name them. Jacey's radar went up. Matt? Was Desi out with Matt Canseco? She was about to find out when her call-waiting beeped in. She checked the number, hoping it was Logan. Had he felt badly after she'd gone? A part of her hoped so.

It wasn't her boyfriend, but the incoming call was from Michigan. "Mom? Larry? Is everything OK? It must be one in the morning!" Jacey said, full of panic.

"We're fine," her stepdad reassured her. "We just wanted to make sure you got back safely, and to see how you made out—all that scrambling!"

"And we didn't even get to see you," her mom said. "Was it worth it?"

Not really, she thought. Not at all. Jacey sighed, and her mom correctly interpreted it. "You can't be all things to all people, my darling daughter. There'll be nothing left for yourself."

"I guess I'm learning," Jacey conceded. "Now, go to bed, both of you."

Jacey sat and surfed the channels, but her thoughts kept drifting back to Logan and how great the prom *hadn't* been. How empty she felt, and stupid, to have gone to such expense and extremes. She ought to have listened to Cinnamon. Even her mom. Logan had not appreciated the humongous effort she'd made just to get there—and not once during the entire night had he told her he loved her.

Jacey picked up her phone and called the delivery service. She wanted chocolate. Now. She ordered a quart of Deep Dark Chocolate Sin ice cream.

Twenty minutes later, she was topping the creamy confection with salty tears. She didn't understand what had happened: she'd tried so hard, pulled off the impossible, and it hadn't been enough. Not for Logan, and worst of all, not for herself.

Eventually, she fell into such a deep sleep, she never heard Ivy, Emilio, Dash, and Aja return.

What woke Jacey was the insistent "Hooray for Hollywood" ring tone of her phone, and then Cinnamon's voice: "Desi's gotta go."

"What?" Jacey said blearily.

"Jacey, wake up. This is Cinnamon, as pissed off as you are to be awakened at four forty-seven in the morning, thanks to the shenanigans of your posse pal."

"Is she okay?" Jacey croaked.

"Desi? Oh, *she's* fine," Cinnamon snarled. "But your image is not, thanks to her. And since you can't seem to housebreak her, I have to be the bad guy and insist you send her packing—back to Michigan."

"Wait—what's she done now?" Jacey sat up in bed.

"What else, you mean, aside from all the public displays of idiocy before tonight?"

Jacey tensed, remembering her friend's vague message. Whom had she been out with tonight?

"You can thank Peyton for putting up bail money," Cinnamon said huffily, "for Desi *and* for her NBF. Your publicist sprung them both."

"Bail money? NBF?" Jacey repeated stupidly.

"New best friend. Gina Valentine."

Jacey BFF in Bar Brawl!
Hauled Off to City Jail!

Jacey's personal assistant, Desiree Paczki (aka Desi) was taken into custody late last night, along with veteran troublemaker and sometime actress Gina Valentine. The party pair were busted during an all-out, fists-flying brawl with alleged drug runners who frequent Dungeon, a well-known den of debauchery! Jacey herself did not show, but it prompts the question: was Desi doing her dirty work, procuring drugs for her? Is this how far America's sweetheart has fallen? In related news, Matt Canseco had his own run-in with the authorities, apparently trying to break up the fight. It's unclear whether charges will be filed against anyone, though all sides have lawyered up. Most interesting tidbit? Jacey's people put up bail money for Desi and Gina.

Chapter Fifteen

You Can't Always Get What You Want

By five thirty in the morning, Peyton delivered Desi to their door. Ivy, Dash, and Jacey were waiting in the foyer.

Desi's head was down, her hands stuffed in her jeans pockets. She looked tinier than ever, ashamed. Jacey's first instinct was to comfort her, tell her it would be all right. Her second instinct was to slug her.

Ivy was boiling, probably because Desi's emergency *du jour* had interrupted her all-night party with Emilio. "What the hell? Do we have to babysit you twenty-four-seven?"

"I'm sorry, guys, it wasn't our fault," Desi mumbled, "but when those creeps got in our faces, when they dissed . . ."

"Rewind, please." Dash broke in. "What were you doing at Dungeon anyway?"

"With Gina Valentine?" Ivy asked accusingly.

"And Matt?" Jacey put in.

The night, according to Desi, had started off innocently enough. Matt had called inviting her to Dungeon with the guys. When they had picked her up in Rob's Escalade, Gina was in the backseat.

"And still you went?" Jacey was incredulous.

"You guys weren't around. I was bored," she whined.

"Are you . . ." Jacey's eyes filled unexpectedly with tears, "with Matt?"

"No way! We're friends, that's all."

Jacey crossed her arms over her chest and sneered. "Really?"

Desi's jaw dropped. "You can't think I'm hooking up with him?"

"Why not? You cashed in your V-card long ago," Jacey said cruelly.

Dash's eyes widened, and Ivy's hand flew to her mouth.

Desi's face crumpled. "You didn't used to be like this, Jace," she murmured.

"Like what?"

"Jealous. Insecure. Paranoid. Nasty."

"Just go on, Desi. Tell us what else," Dash said calmly. "Was anyone doing drugs?"

"That's the thing! We weren't—it was these random jerks next to us who were using. And okay, maybe we were a little loud, but they started dissing us. Trashing Matt, and Gina, and—"

"And you, defender of rich movie stars and their hangers-on, had to fight them?" Ivy snarled.

"*They* started it! Threw drinks at us! Gina got soaked. Rob was a little drunk—it escalated from there. Everyone got into it. I couldn't stand aside."

"Yeah, you could!" Jacey countered. "Did it ever occur to you to whip out that pricey little Razr I got you, and call nine-one-one?"

"Or call a cab!" Ivy exclaimed. "And get your butt out of there?"

"Not when they were trashing my best friend, too." Desi eyed Jacey meaningfully.

"This is like a theme song," Dash muttered, pacing the marble floor.

"Gina defended you, too, Jacey. So did Matt," Desi said pointedly. "That's what friends do."

"Gee, thanks. So Gina Valentine is my friend now? That makes me feel all warm and fuzzy." Jacey stalked away. How could she tell them about Cinnamon's call?

That her agent had ordered her to kick Desi out, send her back to Michigan?

Jacey headed to her rooftop terrace and, without realizing it, turned her face eastward, into the sunrise, toward home. She dropped into the recliner and laced her fingers behind her head. Maybe she wasn't doing Desi any favors by having her out here. Desi never meant any harm, but she just didn't fit in in L.A. She was like the proverbial bull in a china shop. Maybe it would be better if Desi did go back home.

Cinnamon was usually right. She'd guided Jacey through the Hollywood jungle, assembled a team of professionals on Jacey's behalf, advised her, protected her.

Or did Cinnamon have other interests? Like her own? Jacey closed her eyes and willed her mind to go play elsewhere: this sandbox was toxic.

Lost in her thoughts, she never heard a visitor approach.

"Yo, Dimples."

Her heart quickened, her eyes flickered, and Matt Canseco came into view, tanned, toned, wrapped in that beat-up bomber jacket. He was staring down at her. She looked directly into his bittersweet chocolate eyes. Eyes that had stared out from a million movie screens and been open all night, yet, unlike her own, did not betray a trace of fatigue.

"What are you doing here, Matt?"

"Came to check on you."

Jacey hadn't realized she was shivering until Matt slipped out of his jacket and covered her with it.

She tucked it under her chin. The quilted lining was torn, and warm from his body.

"Wanna talk about it?" Matt asked, perching on the low brick wall that surrounded the terrace.

Jacey sat up and searched his face—why was he really there? To defend Desi? Explain his own actions? Was he playing her? Or just playing himself? Could she trust him? She took a chance.

"Cinnamon told me to fire Desi."

Matt blinked. "Fire her? From what? Does she have an actual job, working for you?"

Jacey frowned. He was mocking her.

"It makes no sense," Matt said. "It's not like she's your agent. You can fire your agent, or your publicist. But Hamtramck? She's your—"

"—Friend!" Jacey retorted coldly. "I'm aware."

"So you want to fire her from being your friend?" Matt's tone turned playful.

"Of course not! You're making this sound ridiculous."

"Because it *is* ridiculous. Just wanna make sure you see that."

"Thanks, Mr. Canseco, I can see just fine."

"You're not actually thinking of sending her home?" Matt's prodding unnerved her. "'Cause, according to Hamtramck, meeting you was the best thing that ever happened to her."

Jacey swallowed, a hard knot in her throat. "Desi's always there for me. No way I could do this, be out here, handle all this stuff, without her, Ivy, and Dash. I know that."

"You trust Desi," Matt said as he dragged the blue-and-white-striped chaise lounge over to her. He sat on it sideways, his loafered feet on the ground, facing her. "In this town, people you can trust are few and far between. You gotta hold on to your real friends."

"Desi's naive," Jacey said, more to herself than to Matt. "Overenthusiastic, reckless—"

"She keeps it real," Matt continued. "She doesn't blow smoke. She says what she thinks, does what she thinks is right. That's hard to find around here." Matt made a sweeping gesture with his arm, indicating the pristine neighborhood below them.

"Should I say something to her? Ask her to lay low for a while?" Jacey asked.

"Tell her to stop being who she is? You really want to do that?" Matt leaned toward her slightly. His knees were now touching the side of her recliner.

"Cinnamon says Desi's bad for my image," Jacey confessed nervously.

"Whoa, so let me get this straight. A manufactured image should dictate who your friends are?"

"Of course not! When you put it that way, it sounds stupid. But what about all the people who voted for me on *Generation Next*? They got me where I am. They expect me to be a certain way. Don't I owe them something?"

"They voted for your acting talent, not your sainthood! Besides, how long do you have to be beholden to them? Is there an expiration date or is this a lifetime commitment?"

For the first time in two days, Jacey giggled.

"Here's what you owe them," Matt said. "Your best work. Period."

"Easy for you to say! What would you know about it? Your image—your rep—is an all-access pass to do whatever you want, no consequences!"

"No one forced an image on me, to live up to—or to live down. This is who I am," Matt said. "If you know who you are, decisions come easy."

"What if I'm not sure?" She gulped, embarrassed, and looked away from him, mumbling, "I used to know. I was just Jacey, this girl from Bloomfield Hills. But now that I'm here, listening to what everybody says about me, writes about me, tells me what to do, I'm not sure anymore."

"Then figure it out."

Jacey turned back and gazed at him.

Matt reached over and took her hands in his. Her skin prickled. It was all she could do not to leap up and fling herself into his arms.

"Can you help me?" she said, trembling.

"Me? No. But you could start by asking yourself what's keeping you here? The money, designer clothes, big fancy house, getting pampered, having fans, all the freebies . . ." he trailed off.

"I don't know what you mean." Jacey squirmed uncomfortably, slipping her hands out from under his. Was he judging her?

"You know exactly what I mean, Dimples. Would you stay here if every movie you made was *Galaxy Rangers*?"

She colored. What had he heard? "Ouch."

Matt softened. "Sorry, sometimes I forget you're a newbie. And I wouldn't say this if I didn't believe it—but I watched you on *Generation Next*. . . ."

He had? She lit up. "You did? Did you vote—?"

Matt didn't answer. Instead he prodded, "Look, Jacey, do you really want to be an actor? Or is it cool with you just to be a starlet?"

"Can't I be both?"

"Do you want to get better at your craft, or skate along as this really hot starlet who sometimes stumbles into great movies, like *Four Sisters*?

Matt thought she was hot?

"When people go to your movies," he continued, "do you want them to see the character, or you? Do you want to be Julia Roberts, where you know it's her up on the screen no matter if she's playing in *Erin Brockovich* or *Pretty Woman*? Or someone who disappears into her character, like Catherine Keener or Evan Rachel Wood? 'Cause, if you're asking me, at this point you could go either way."

"It's more complicated for me than for you, Matt." Jacey set her jaw.

"Not really. I have a reputation, you have an image. I got it because I don't play the Hollywood game. I take roles in movies that say something to me, that I connect with. I don't care if people like my character: if it touches me, if it means something to me, I gotta figure it'll touch others, too."

"Like the movie you're doing now, *Dirt Nap*? What's it about?"

"I play this rich kid, William Soloway, heir to a drug company fortune, straitlaced, uptight, all Harvard Business School."

"Really? That's so not you!" Jacey could *not* picture Matt in that role.

"Wait, let me finish," he said. "He's a golden boy with a perfect life. Then his best friend dies, from a drug overdose. He finds out that the drug was made by his dad's company, and they knew—and covered up—the deadly side effects and risks, and continued to market it."

"What does William do?" Jacey was instantly drawn into the story.

"That's the thing. Instead of being a whistle-blower, putting his dad out of business, torpedoing his own fortune—or just turning a blind eye to it—he runs. Takes off, leaves everything, changes his name and appearance, vanishes where no one can find him."

"Obviously, someone does," Jacey guessed.

"He ends up in this rural outpost somewhere in Appalachia. He meets a waitress, Sarah—his complete opposite. Somehow, they forge a bond."

"And she leads him to redemption?"

"Ha! No way!" Matt's eyes sparkled. "That's where it gets interesting. Slowly, we find out that Sarah's not quite the sweet, innocent, poor girl William thinks she is. She's greedy, sneaky, bad to the bone, and little by little, turns him upside down. Scams him—eventually, tries to kill him."

Now Jacey was really intrigued. "What happens in the end?"

"Willy learns the hard way that greed has many faces, and he can't run away from it. The best he can do . . . if he survives . . ." Matt said, "is decide how he wants to live his life, what kind of man he wants to be."

"Wow! Cool!" Jacey's mind was racing, trying again to picture Matt in the role.

"It's one kid's journey. There's no special effects, no A-list stars."

"But it speaks to you," she mused. "I can see why."

"It's about hard choices. And besides, I want to work with the guy who's directing it."

"Right," Jacey said slowly. Noel Langer. The one who doubted her talent. The one person at her afterparty who hadn't wanted to take a meeting with her.

"So, who's playing Sarah?" Jacey asked.

"They're casting now."

"Oh. My. God." Jacey paused dramatically between each word. "I so have to do this role. I *get* this girl."

"You do?" Ivy challenged, her face a worried frown. "She's a greedy backstabber."

"Who isn't even pretty," Desi put in.

Two days after Jacey's eye-opening talk with Matt,

everyone gathered in the spa bathroom to do a read-aloud of *Dirt Nap*. After much cajoling, Jacey had gotten Matt to lend her the script. He'd questioned her sincerity about wanting to audition, but after his little speech about meaningful roles, he'd hardly been able to turn down her request.

Jacey smiled to herself, remembering the backpedaling he'd done: "Trying out for an indie just to disprove your image is as bad as sticking with wholesome roles— you're still reacting to other people's perceptions of you."

"I'd like my next movie to be interesting," she'd explained. "Unlike *Galaxy Rangers*, which is, as you've read, a suckfest."

"—But it's *your* suckfest," Matt had pointed out. "No one forced you into it. You chose it. And so what? We all make dumb-ass choices sometimes. Then you move on."

"Let me read *Dirt Nap*," she'd said. "I promise not to try out unless I honestly connect with Sarah."

"Sarah's a conniving bitch. She never redeems herself," Dash was saying.

"Not in the script, no," Jacey conceded.

"She's there only so William learns his lesson," Ivy said. "She's one-dimensional."

Jacey smiled craftily. "And that's where I come in. I can make the audience understand why she's like that, so even if you don't like her, you *get* her."

"Not." Ivy shook her head. "Getting. It."

"It's called acting," said Jacey with a wink. She sailed out of the room, clutching the script to her chest. This was cool. *This* was the reason she was there. All she had to do was convince Cinnamon to get her an audition, which might have to be the performance of a lifetime!

Jacey had not responded to Cinnamon's dump-Desi demand. She'd asked for time, and for once, time had been on her side. The *Seventeen* magazine article came out. It featured a glowing portrait of Jacey the actress, *and* Jacey the person!

On the cover, they had used the picture of her in the Swarovski studded jeans and Bisou Bisou flowy halter top. Her hair was wavy, her makeup subtle, her smile genuine. The article covered her childhood, her love for acting, the way she'd felt when she won *Generation Next*, and the time when she'd launched her career with *Four Sisters*.

The main focus, however, was on Jacey's best trait: her loyalty to her old friends Dash Walker (no mention was made of his sexuality), Ivy Langhorne, and bubbly Desiree Paczki. The article managed to make Jacey look like America's sweetheart *and* America's real deal, a certifiable new star *in* Hollywood, who would never *go* Hollywood.

No way could Cinnamon make Jacey dump Desi now. How would that look? What would the blogger say? Jacey's best face forward was face out on magazine stands all over the country. Cinnamon's phone rang off the hook with compliments; her e-mailbox piled up with offers. A big publishing company wanted Jacey to write her autobiography. A perfume company wanted to manufacture her scent. She was asked to be a character in a video game and to lend her name to a line of clothes.

It was the perfect time for Jacey to ask Cinnamon for what she wanted.

"It's *fabulous!*" Cinnamon gushed, rereading select paragraphs over bagels and lox at Barney Greengrass, the chichi rooftop eatery above Barneys, overlooking Rodeo Drive. "This article exposes the blog as bogus, and reinforces the reason you were named America's Top Young Actress. It reminds the voters they were right about you."

"I have an even better way to remind them." Jacey had practiced what she was going to say. Cinnamon wasn't going to like it, which was the real reason Jacey had suggested lunch, just the two of them. Her agent could hardly pitch a fit in public.

"Let's hear it," Cinnamon said enthusiastically, spreading a thick layer of no-carb, low-fat, cream cheese on the whole wheat bagel she'd scooped the bread out of.

"I want you to get me an audition for my next movie."

"Of course I will. As soon as *Galaxy* wraps, we're on it." She bit into her bagel.

Jacey pulled the script out of her Marc Jacobs satchel. "They're casting now."

Cinnamon's stopped in midchew, picked up a napkin, and wiped her mouth. "What is this? *Dirt Nap*? Never heard of it. Besides—it'll never sell with that title."

"And yet, killer plot." Jacey's eyes sparkled as she began to describe the picture.

Cinnamon looked suspicious. "Please don't tell me Matt Canseco has anything to do with this."

Jacey had anticipated a struggle—over the indie thing and over the idea of playing an unlikable character. She hadn't counted on Matt's being the obstacle. She should have. Cinnamon had never hidden her disdain for him.

"He's pushing you to do this, isn't he?"

"Not even," Jacey countered. "I had to beg him for a copy of the script."

"I see," Cinnamon said. "So you're letting a crush dictate which movies you go out for."

Jacey's jaw tightened. "That's unfair. And just plain wrong. If you read the script you'll see—"

"I have no intention of reading it." Cinnamon waved dismissively.

"Then have your people read it." Jacey wouldn't be dissuaded. "Ask them what they really think of it, not if they'd recommend it for a Jacey Chandliss movie. And don't forget that in *Generation Next*, I played unlikable characters sometimes. And people still voted for me."

"There's a big difference between doing a skit on a TV show and acting in a movie that you'll be remembered for, that will forever be part of your body of work. That will come back to haunt you."

"It's a chance I'm willing to take." Jacey was steadfast. "I'm asking you, as my agent, and as someone who cares about me, to let me take it."

Cinnamon was stymied. Her patented *"fabulous!"* for once didn't work.

"Noel Langer may not want to see you."

"Then make him," Jacey told her. "You can do this. You're Cinnamon T. Jones."

Jacey Robbed of Prom Queen Crown!

Call it karma, or maybe Gina Valentine had a vote—but really, how did Jacey *not* get crowned queen at her high school prom? Especially when her back-home boyfriend snared king. Who's more popular than Jacey? Oh, wait—just about any other senior at her alma mater! But I digress. So picture this: there she is, big Hollywood star in her scarlet designer gown, standing there, all alone, watching another girl wear her tiara, and dance in the arms of her boyfriend.

Cue the violins!

Chapter Sixteen

The Happiest Place on Earth

"This is so fun!" Desi shrieked. "I always dreamed about coming here!"

The weekend following Jacey's lunch with Cinnamon, Peyton had called with a cool offer: "You've been invited to a VIP day at Disneyland. Everything's complimentary, you can go on as many rides as you want—you jump all the lines. They provide bodyguards so no one bothers you."

The catch was that Jacey had to pose for pictures as she rode Space Mountain. The photos would be taken by Disneyland's official photographer, to be distributed to major magazines and Web sites.

"They do it all the time, with lots of celebrities,"

Peyton had explained. "It's good publicity, win-win."

Taking Desi along was perfect. It gave her some alone time with the Master of *Des*-aster, as Dash had taken to calling her.

Jacey's mood had lifted, thanks to Matt Canseco and *Dirt Nap*. She hadn't heard from her agent yet, but Cinnamon would come through, Jacey was certain of it. Because, as she'd excitedly explained to the posse, "in her heart—deep down—Cinn believes in me."

"Or, believes that no way you're gonna get this part, so no harm, no foul," the doubting Dash had speculated.

"Or, she works for you, and you can fire her if she doesn't come through," Ivy had added.

Jacey had grimaced. She had never told Ivy or Dash about Cinnamon's order to fire Desi. It was July, and they'd been in L.A. for over three months. Although they'd made other connections, her posse had grown tighter, not just with her, but with each other. Dash, Ivy, and Jacey vowed to defend Desi if Dungeon decided to file charges against her. Behind the scenes, Dash and Ivy paid for damages and then some to incentivize the club's owners not to.

They put aside other plans to help Jacey rehearse for her hoped-for *Dirt Nap* audition. They went over the script multiple times, allowing her to test different ways of portraying Sarah. When they liked her interpretation, they cheered. If she hit a wrong note, if a scene stank—they jeered.

There was no better audience, no better friends.

As she and Desi ducked into Sleeping Beauty Castle, Jacey hugged her friend.

"What was that for?" Desi asked, obviously pleased.

"For being you, that's all," Jacey smiled.

"I guess this means you forgive me," Desi said with a sly grin. "You know I would never do anything purposely to embarrass you, Jace."

"Nor I you," Jacey replied soberly. "Not that you make it easy! Seriously, Des, don't ever change. Even if what you do does embarrass me."

"So you're giving me free rein to keep *you* real?" Desi's eyes twinkled mischievously.

"Only if you stop crashing my cars!" Jacey elbowed her, and they burst out laughing.

"Hey, you never got to tell me what happened at the prom," Desi said. "The only place I can get any info is your fan blog. Where I learned you didn't make prom queen. Sorry 'bout that. Anything else you care to share?"

Jacey's smile faded. So did her high spirits. "It just wasn't what I thought it would be."

"Could ya vague that up a little more?" Desi quipped. "Was it the prom itself, the kids, your parents, being home? Logan? What disappointed you?"

"Other way around," Jacey said with a sigh. "I felt like I disappointed everyone."

"Not possible!" Desi cried. "You did everything right. You nearly killed yourself, and all of us, getting there. And you looked amazing, sprinkled with movie-star dust. Who said you disappointed them, anyway?" Desi balled up her fists and joshed, "I'll take out a hit on them. . . ."

Jacey grinned appreciatively. "No one said it in so many words. But I know my parents felt shortchanged. I didn't get to see them at all! A bunch of kids at the prom called me a diva 'cause we got there so late, and others just wanted to know about Hollywood stuff. It just wasn't fun—I had to leave before breakfast. And Logan? I dunno, he felt—"

Desi stopped her. "Not asking how he felt. How'd you feel?"

"I felt . . . nothing. How weird is that?"

At that exact moment, both their cell phones rang, and the girls jumped.

"Logan," Jacey said, answering her phone and feigning enthusiasm. "How are you?"

"Hey, Matt," Desi said with a grin, "Jacey and I are at Disneyland! Yeah, I know it's cheesy. Cheesy-cool!"

Logan was returning Jacey's call . . . after she had

returned his call. Or something. Jacey was no longer sure who'd left the last message, only that they'd barely spoken since the prom—and not at all about the night itself. And now was not the time or the place. So she talked about taking Desi to Disneyland, and he told her about everyone's summer plans. They hung up, having done little more than trade info.

When Desi closed her phone, Jacey folded her arms. "Truth. Are you and Matt a thing?"

"No! Matt is a cool guy. He's fun, adventurous. He listens when you talk—he's a movie star; I'm . . . well . . . not. What's cool is that he doesn't act like a high-and-mighty movie star. He doesn't condescend, y'know? We're friends, that's all." Desi did not sound the least bit defensive.

"And yet, if you wanted to go after him . . ." Jacey paused. "Not that you need my blessing, but you have it. If you and Matt have a connection, if you want more, go for it. It won't ruin our friendship."

Desi pursed her lips, then paused. "It's not me he's interested in."

"What do you know?" Jacey grabbed Desi's arm.

Desi would have answered, but she didn't get the chance. Jacey's phone started to play "Hooray for Hollywood," and the screen signaled a text message from Cinnamon. *GT U audition!*

"Whoo-hoo, YES!" Desi screamed and clapped, eyeing the screen along with Jacey.

Jacey finished reading and started hyperventilating. "Oh, no! I have to be there in two hours! I'm not ready! We'll never make it."

"You are, and you will. You know you can do this." With that, Desi called for the limo.

"You do realize, Miss Chandliss, that few audiences ever see independent movies," Noel Langer said.

"Unless they turn out to be *March of the Penguins*, or *The Blair Witch Project*," Jacey replied with a friendly smile. Her heart was beating so loudly she was sure everyone in the room could hear—she remembered her nervous palpitations during the *Gen Next* finals. Only, back then, she was in a studio overflowing with fans, judges, celebrities, and a live band.

Here, there were half a dozen people crowded into the small living room of someone's cottage in Santa Monica, among them the director who had doubted her talent: Noel Langer. Plus, three producers and the casting agent.

"Do you think *Dirt Nap* will turn out to be a sleeper?" Noel asked pointedly. "Is that why you want to audition?"

Oy. She was auditioning to audition! Jacey had to

convince them that she was serious, that this wasn't just a lark. She raised her chin slightly and looked straight at Noel. "I was given the opportunity to read the script, and I thought it was an amazing piece," she answered honestly. "I related to the hard choices these characters have to make."

"Actors on this film are paid only scale, no matter what contest they won. Do you understand that?" the executive producer asked with a scowl.

"Yes, I do, sir," Jacey responded calmly.

"You won't have a fancy trailer—you may not have a private dressing room at all. There won't be room in the budget for star perks," mentioned the associate producer, a balding guy trying to cover it up with a comb-over.

"I don't need star perks," Jacey said quietly. "I'd like the opportunity to be part of a wonderful piece of story-telling."

The line producer, a jowly British guy, cleared his throat. "One must applaud your bravery, then. To tackle such a hateful, spiteful character—are you quite sure you want to do this? From what I read, aren't you America's newest little sweetheart?"

"Yes, won't you care if audiences turn on you?" asked the executive producer.

"I care," she said carefully, "if I give them a bad

performance. Then there's a reason for them to, as you say, turn on me. But if I do my job, if I bring a character to life—I'm fine with however audiences see me."

"A dangerous move," she overheard Scowly mumble to Baldy.

"Dangerous, or gutsy?" Noel, the director, wondered out loud.

"I'd like to thank you for the chance to try out." Jacey had learned a thing or two from Peyton—"I know you're busy and you have doubts about me. I don't know if I'm what you're looking for in Sarah, but I do promise not to waste your time."

Noel smiled. Jacey totally caught it. Okay, she'd charmed the director. Let's see if she could wow him.

"You'll start with Sarah's scene on page forty seven," Noel instructed. "Our casting guru, Janice, will read the part of your half sister, Wanda."

Jacey had struggled with that scene while rehearsing. In it, Sarah was unjustifiably mean to her younger, better-looking sibling. She'd read it over several times, with Desi and Ivy taking turns as Wanda, and she'd never really been happy with her performance. Starting with this scene was tough.

Only, something happened just then, standing in the middle of that wood-paneled living room, face to face with

Janice, the casting director. Suddenly, she saw Wanda through Sarah's eyes: that girl was a threat to her, and could derail the scheme she had envisioned. Jacey performed the scene in a completely new way.

"Well done!" Noel marveled, when she'd finished. He sounded surprised.

The executive producer gave a curt nod.

"We have several other scenes to try," said Jowly. "Mr. Canseco, would you please read with Miss Chandliss?"

Jacey had not noticed Matt enter the room. She forced herself not to react. She noted immediately that Matt's normal, loping gait had become stiffer, more formal, as he approached. He gave no sign he'd ever met her before.

Then again, the character he was portraying, William Soloway, had not. And it was preppy, confused, tortured William who stood before her. Before Sarah, the wily scam artist.

The air between them was electric.

In their first scene, as William and Sarah conversed, sparks flew! And in the second scene, as she teared up in a bid to win his sympathy, and in the third scene, as she dried his tears while he told her about his best friend's demise.

In the final scene of the audition, they gazed into each other's eyes. . . . It was magical.

Everyone in the room knew it. Even Scowly burst into spontaneous applause, along with the rest of the group. Their reaction jolted Jacey back to reality. Instinctively, she pulled away from Matt, flustered.

Matt was smiling broadly. He slipped an arm around her waist, gave her a peck on the cheek. "You did good, Dimples."

Noel, the producers, and the casting agent surrounded her, brimming with compliments. "We're not allowed to say anything," Noel whispered, "but you can bet we'll be calling your agent the minute you leave the room!"

Jacey Takes a Dirt Nap!
Turns Her Back on Her Fans?

In a move so under the radar hardly anyone noticed, wholesome Jacey auditioned for a violent, gory, independent movie—where, get this, she'll play a loathsome character. Could this be boyfriend Matt Canseco's influence? 'Cause it just so happens, he's the male lead.

All I can say, Jace, is: bad move! No one wants to see you play evil—no matter what you're doing in real life!

Chapter Seventeen

It's My Party!

"We're so having a par-tay! A par-tay for the part *aced* by Jace! We're celebrating!" Ivy goofily sang and danced her way up to the bar at the roped-off VIP section of Mood.

Cinnamon had called early that morning, confirming she'd gotten a verbal, informal offer for Jacey to star as Sarah in *Dirt Nap*. "Details still have to be worked out," Cinnamon had cautioned. "It's not a signed, sealed, and delivered deal, but we have a firm verbal offer in hand. I knew you'd want to hear right away." That she didn't punctuate her message with *"Fabulous!"* was lost on everyone but Jacey.

Mood had been Ivy's choice. Previous visits had assured her its VIP area boasted the best security around, and the burliest bouncers. This was going to be the first no-holds-barred, no-paparazzi, posse party—it was going to rock the casbah!

Everyone who mattered in young Hollywood, along with their entourages, would be there. Jacey's posse had personally invited Matt, Rob, Emilio, and Aja, and, just because Jacey was feeling generous, even Gina Valentine and her sisters-in-sleaze were on the list. Jacey expected that Adam Pratt would find a way in, too.

For the occasion, Jacey had found an awesome candy-colored flirty Marc Jacobs baby-doll dress. She had added oversize vintage Chanel earrings, a triple-stranded necklace with a green beryl disk, and Prada raggia slides for dancing. In the mood for long hair, she'd spent several hours and several hundreds of dollars having Yuki put golden extensions in her shoulder-length hair, extensions that would have to come out when she reported for work on *Galaxy* the next day, as Zorina wore her hair short, spiky, and gelled.

Jacey rationalized that this was her night. She was in boyfriend flux, and she could afford it. She sashayed up to the bar and gave Ivy a quick hug.

"You're the best, Cuz," she said.

"And don't you forget it," Ivy replied jauntily.

"What's your pleasure, ladies?" asked the bartender.

"Our special cocktail tonight is a *Dirt Nap* martini. It's vodka, olive juice, and tiny chocolate shavings."

Jacey was impressed. Ivy had outdone herself: the finger-food menu featured "dirt" sandwiches; the drinks included "dirty" margaritas and daiquiris; and bunches of flowers and balloon bouquets dotted the room.

Partygoers crowded around Jacey. Unlike the people at the prom, these were industry people, insiders, who didn't squeal and ask if Target sold that bag, or beg to try on her shoes! The attention made her feel like a star, like one of them.

The DJ, sequestered inside a glass booth, kept the music cranked, and by eleven, the time of the e-vite, the place was packed with famous faces and 300-sit-ups-a-day bods gyrating to the thumping rhythm, bumping hips, writhing suggestively, throwing back shots, laughing, and—in some cases—seriously canoodling. As anticipated, young Hollywood (and Jacey was part of it) had left its inhibitions at the door, along with cameras. It was beyond cool.

Matt hadn't shown up yet, but Jacey knew he would—they'd be costarring in *Dirt Nap*!

Jacey also had a couple of calls out to Logan, not only to share her exciting news, but to see if, now that school was over, he'd come to L.A. Maybe it had been missed signals and circumstances that had led to their disconnect at the prom. Maybe if Logan came here, they could get back on track. "It's worth a try," agreed Desi when she told her.

Ivy waved at her from the end of the bar. Jacey held up her empty martini glass, signaling that she'd like another.

Good thing, too: she needed a second at just that moment.

"So, congratulations," Sierra Tucson, her jealous *Four Sisters* costar said, easing up to the bar. "Word is, you snagged, what, some low-budget indie? That's so brave!"

Jacey took in Sierra's plunging minidress, sashed waist, and steel-toed stilettos. Pushing through the crowd to catch up with Sierra was Kate Summers, covered in a spray-on tan and lots of bling. A *Four Sisters* reunion, Jacey thought, tipping back her head to pour her drink straight down, with the two costars she had hoped to never see again.

"So lovely of you to come," Jacey said in her best phony voice. "What are you drinking? It's on me."

"So generous," said Kate, "but you don't need to pretend with us. We're your friends. And from the awful buzz about *Galaxy Rangers* . . ." She paused. "I hope you weren't counting on back-end money? I doubt there'll be any."

"And God knows what pittance they're paying you for

that indie," Sierra sniffed. "You should save your money."

"Did you two just come from a hookup with my accountant?" Jacey asked, amused. "Surely I can afford to be generous, especially with my dearest *old* costars. Have either of you landed a new gig yet?" She held her martini glass up and crossed her legs, pretending to look interested.

"Sweetie, don't be like that. We're just trying to help. It's sad to see such a promising career being flushed down the toilet." Sierra touched Jacey's arm.

"Whose career is in the crapper? Sierra's or Kate's?" Dash, munching on a minicaviar wrap, sauntered over at just the right moment.

Jacey giggled, while Kate fumed and Sierra huffed.

"Why don't you go help yourself to some caviar? Savor the hors d'oeuvres; they're killer, and compliments of Jacey." Dash shooed them away.

"Unfortunately, there are no cameras allowed," Jacey tossed in, as Kate and Sierra turned to leave. "You won't be able to elbow me out of any pictures tonight."

She and Dash did a high five. "How'd the Desperate Wannabes get in?" Jacey asked.

"According to them, they're your best friends," Dash shrugged. "Especially when there's free food."

Randee Bleich, a newcomer who'd just landed a role

on a new TV show, zeroed in on Jacey's new Hermès Birkin bag in lime. "How'd you get it? The list is, like, months long!"

The girl was plastered, and so was her best friend, another teen actress named Sandra, or Sandee.

"The designer sent it over," Jacey explained. "It's my new favorite accessory—it holds everything. Wanna see?"

"They sent it to you?" Randee was dumbfounded. "No way! I am so firing my agent for not getting me this!"

Jacey opened the satchel to show the awestruck girls. Suddenly her cell phone began to vibrate. She grabbed it and checked the caller ID.

She mimed to Randee and Sandee that she needed to take the call, and hopped off the bar stool, heading toward the privacy of the ladies' room.

"Logan! What fabulous timing—I was trying to get away from these two. . . ." She paused, realizing he hadn't said anything; had she lost the call?

"Logan, are you there? Can you hear me?"

"Yeah, Jacey. I hear you fine."

"Oh, my God, it must be what, three in the morning back there?" Jacey cried.

"Somethin' like that," Logan said. "Just got in, and saw you called. What's up?"

What's up? Not . . . hi, how are you? Not, congratulations

on *Dirt Nap*? "Did you get my text message?" she asked.

He hesitated, as if trying to remember. "The one about the dirty something?"

"Cinnamon said it's in the bag, they loved me—isn't that cool?" Jacey explained about the movie, slowly realizing Logan wasn't interested. He didn't get what this meant to her. Or, worse, he did—and didn't care.

"Hey, Lo," she said. "I also left a message about you coming out here. You have time now."

"Jacey, I can't, you know that. I have a job."

"And that takes up twenty-four-seven? C'mon, what about . . . your . . . um, social life? You've gotta have time for that."

"Are you kidding? I go out all the time. In fact, I just got in. A bunch of us went to a party." He hiccupped.

Was it possible? She nearly kicked herself—here she was in the middle of her own A-list showbiz fiesta: Lindsay was on the dance floor, Ashlee was crooning in some cute guy's ear, Desi was sharing a joke with *American Idol*'s Taylor—the entire cast of *Smallville* had come to congratulate her, and she felt—*left out*?

Jacey couldn't help herself. "Who had the party?"

There was silence on the other end. Had she lost him?

She braced herself. "Tiffany? Was it at her house, Logan?"

"No, it was at Tyler's house—and a lot of people were there. Speaking of—it sounds noisy where you are. What're you doing?"

"Celebrating me getting the role," she replied, as brightly as possible, "and wishing you were here to celebrate with me."

"I'm sure I'll read all about it in tomorrow's blog."

Had Logan really said that? Jacey was caught off guard. Before she had a chance to recover, Logan was ready to get off the phone. "G'night, Jacey. I'm wiped. We'll talk later."

Jacey fought back the hard knot of tears and opened the ladies' room door. Ivilio—Jacey had taken to thinking of them as one entity—was laughing loudly behind a closed stall.

Jacey turned the cold water on full strength and faced herself in the mirror. Her stormy-ocean eyes, rimmed in charcoal, were wet with tears. Her pouty lips needed gloss; her cheeks screamed for blush. Unfortunately, all her makeup was in her Hermès bag, which she'd left by the bar with Randee and Sandee.

What was wrong with her? She should have been having an awesome time. She had been, too—before Logan called. Why was it that lately, every time she talked to him, it brought her down?

The giggling from inside the closed stall had morphed into heavy breathing. Time to go. Jacey tucked the hair extensions behind her ear, dabbed her eyes carefully with a tissue, and headed back to her party.

A blast of loud music hit her full force as she exited the ladies' room and ran straight into Desi.

"You okay?" Desi asked. Sweat poured down her flushed face. "Couldn't find you for a while."

"I'm good." She signaled to the bartender. "About to be better."

Desi grinned. "I'll drink to that!" Fueled up, the girls hit the dance floor.

Jacey proceeded to dance—with guys, with groups of girls, even solo—she didn't care what she looked like or who saw her. If Jacey was overcompensating, forcing herself not to think about Logan, no one noticed. Certainly not Desi, who'd gotten on top of a table for a dance smackdown against a bunch of blinged-out girls.

Dash hadn't observed Jacey dancing energetically. He was schmoozing the room.

Jacey looked for Ivy. Was her cousin still in the ladies' room with Emilio? Just then, Ivy emerged. Jacey rushed over and pushed her back inside.

"What's the matter?" Ivy asked.

"Your frock, cuzzie-bear, is on backward!"

Ivy looked down. "Oh, damn!" The buttons were in the front, the plunging neckline in back. "How'd that happen?"

She and Jacey burst out laughing.

"Thanks for not giving me up," Ivy said between guffaws, "I love you, little cuzzie."

"Love you, too. Ives. Thanks for this . . . party—this everything. You're the best."

Desi teetered into the bathroom. "Gotta go, gotta go, gotta—what're you two doing here?"

"Making a few adjustments," Jacey giggled, "and reminding myself who my real friends are. Go, *you*, for showing 'em how tabletop dancing is done!"

Desi dashed into the stall, howling with laughter.

When Jacey reemerged into the room the party had amped up. Dirty-dancing, loud music, and a hot crowd had translated into one rockin' scene.

The person Jacey wanted most to see, however, was not there. Matt Canseco had yet to show.

And the last person she wanted in her face was there. "So," Adam Pratt drawled into her ear, "I hear congrats are in order. I hope your little indie adventure isn't taking your mind off our *major* motion picture."

Jacey didn't respond.

"Did Emory tell you? We're gonna have to redo our love scene." Adam gave her a sly look.

"Tell me this is your idea of a joke, Adam."

"Your fault," he said, then slurped his drink. "You sleepwalked through it last week."

"Oh, give me a break," she groaned.

"Wanna practice now?" he pulled her close. "You look good enough to eat, my sensuous costar."

"As if." She started to turn on her heel and walk away, but the DJ had just switched to a slow song, and Adam's arms were around her before she could protest. He pulled her close and started to slow-dance. She tensed.

"Come on, Jacey, lighten up," Adam whispered in her ear. "It's a party—your party, and I don't see you with a boyfriend. You're the woman of the hour, and all alone. We can fix that, starting now."

It was all Jacey could do to not hurl. Fine, she'd let him have one dance. It didn't mean she had to listen to him. But Adam kept needling her. "Didn't the prom turn out to be your special night? How come prom boy's not here?"

No way was Jacey giving Adam the satisfaction of finding out how awful the prom had been, what a great big disappointment. She simply tossed her head and prayed the song would end soon.

"Know what I think?" Adam nibbled her earlobe playfully. "I think you need a boyfriend in the industry, an actor. Someone who understands the demands your career makes."

"Know what I think?" The voice was deep, strong, sure. And achingly familiar. "I think Ms. Chandliss is ready for a new dance partner." Matt Canseco carefully removed Adam's arms from around Jacey.

Adam sized Matt up for one fleeting second, as if he were going to challenge the bigger, tougher guy. He decided to back off.

Jacey exhaled, melting into Matt's arms. "Thank you."

"For what?" Matt said.

"Being here," she said honestly. "I know this place isn't your scene."

"What could I do? My posse's here, and so, I hear, is my costar." His smile was electric. It turned Matt Canseco, tough guy, intense brooder, into someone softer, someone vulnerable.

"Are you surprised I got the role?" she asked, hoping they could keep dancing, though the song had changed.

"Not after the audition, no."

Satisfaction spread through Jacey as she rested her head on his shoulder. Somehow, they fit together snugly. Matt was shorter, more compact than Logan. When she and Logan danced, her head rested on his chest. With Matt, she made it up to his shoulder, where she took in that woodsy aftershave. If it'd been Logan, she would have smooched his neck. But it wasn't, and she wasn't that drunk.

Desi, on the way to being fully sloshed, danced over to them. "You're here! I'm so pumped!"

Was Matt going to slow-dance with her now? The music switched back to dance-club, and Matt gave Desi a squeeze and ambled over to the bar.

"You should table-dance, Jace," Desi said, "It's so fun!"

Jacey considered it. She rocked her dress. There were no paparazzi. And Matt was there.

She and Desi climbed atop a middle table, and started dancing, to enthusiastic applause and garrulous toasts. Someone handed Jacey another drink; it was, she found, easy to dance and drink at the same time. Then she spied Matt—definitely watching her. She shot him a megawatt smile and a wink.

It would be her last genuine smile of the night.

For that was the exact moment the whole scene turned into a blur. She saw Dash rushing, pushing through the crowd, intent on getting to her. Did he want to table-dance, too? The thought sped by as Desi shouted, "Look, Cinnamon is here! How cool is that?"

Jacey's arms were up in the air, her hips undulating. Why was Cinnamon wearing a coat? Sure, it was Prada, but it *so* didn't fit in a place like Mood. At 4 a.m.

Dash was trying to tell her something. So was Cinnamon.

"Can't hear you," Jacey bellowed, kicking up her heels. "I'm dancing!"

If she'd been a lip-reader, perhaps she might've saved herself from what was about to follow. Or, if Cinnamon hadn't been so tired and frustrated, she might not have been shouting; and the entire dance floor, including Matt Canseco, wouldn't have heard her pronouncement.

But, in an epic moment of bad timing, in one split second while the DJ was finding another record and the music stopped, Cinnamon bellowed, "You didn't get the role!"

Then the agent, mortified, realizing that everyone had heard her, clapped her hand over her mouth. Talk about a buzz kill. The sound of A-list jaws dropping was not covered up by the sound of the music starting up again.

If the scene had been scripted, Jacey might have been able to hold on to some dignity. Instead, her knees buckled, and she vomited.

Cinnamon hurried Jacey and her friends out of the club. Next door, at the Coffee Beanery—over Desi's "It's a mistake," and Dash's stunned "This can't be," and Ivy's "I don't understand," and Jacey's "They told me I had it. You told me I had it,"—a sorry, sad, and notably makeup-less Cinnamon delivered the rest of the news.

"Mr. Langer—Noel—loved Jacey's work. So did the producers and casting agents. They were about to send contracts over with the official offer for the part, just like I told you. Only, they got a call from the studio—the studio that's putting up the money to make *Dirt Nap*."

"Some executive at the studio didn't like Jacey?" Dash asked incredulously.

"They weren't even at the audition," Desi protested.

"It wasn't that," Cinnamon explained. "They just decided to cast someone else as Sarah—they forced the decision on Noel."

"Why?" Ivy asked.

"They decided to go with an unknown."

"Who?" asked Jacey, wiping away tears.

Cinnamon looked sick. "The producer's daughter."

Chapter Eighteen

The Boy Who Gets Her . . .

"But that's like insider trading!" Desi protested. "It's illegal!"

The next day, Jacey and the group, stunned and mortified, were on a conference call with Cinnamon.

"It's not illegal, Desi," Cinnamon said wearily. "It's showbiz."

"It's payola!" Desi blurted, trying on every negative showbiz term she could think of—whether or not it made any sense.

"It's plain old nepotism, kids," Cinnamon said.

"It's *Galaxy Rangers*, isn't it?" Dash put it together first. "The studio believes the bad buzz."

"They're worried," Cinnamon conceded.

"But no one's seen *Galaxy Rangers*. How could they make decisions on something no one's seen?" Desi asked.

"Buzz is like a deity in this town; everyone believes in it, worships it—good, or bad," Cinnamon replied. "When it was good about *Four Sisters*, it worked for us. If it isn't good . . . it works against us. That's why it's so important for Jacey to keep her image up."

"There's no way to convince them *Galaxy* won't flop and Jacey will remain a huge star?" Dash asked.

"It *will* flop," Jacey put in miserably. Her shoulders sagged. Worst of all? She had so known it all along. She had known it when she read the script; she had known it the first day she started filming. Over the course of the last month, it had only gotten worse, not better.

"But how will it help to have an unknown in the role?" Ivy demanded. "I still don't get it."

An audible sigh came from the other end of the phone. "It doesn't matter whether we understand it or not. Jacey's out. It's a done deal."

"So there's no way you can fix this? Get Jacey her part back?" Dash asked.

"Not this time. All we can do is remain positive, make the best of *Galaxy*, then move on to the next great role."

"Are you even upset, Cinn?" Jacey challenged her.

Cinnamon sighed. "I'm trying to see the bigger picture. So should you."

"You didn't want me to try out for *Dirt Nap*. You thought Matt was influencing me. I can't help thinking you're relieved that I didn't get it in the end."

"You're my client, Jacey. Part of my job is advising you, but another is doing my best to get you what you want, whether I agree professionally or not. I used my influence to get you the audition. But I don't run Hollywood. There's nothing I can do when casting decisions are overruled by studio bosses."

Jacey was still boiling. If there was nothing Cinnamon the Great could do, maybe there was someone else who could.

She grabbed the car keys and bolted.

Matt Canseco answered the door himself. Bed-head hair and overnight stubble told Jacey she'd probably woken him. She glanced at her watch. It wasn't even nine in the morning. And who knew how late he'd been out the previous night?

"Jacey." Matt ran his fingers through his wayward hair and yawned. "Guess I know why you're here. Come on in."

Jacey trailed after him into the small, dark cottage.

Matt motioned toward a sagging, seen-better-days couch. "You want coffee?"

"No, thanks," Jacey responded. "I'm sorry I barged in, but—"

He held his palm up. "Wait. Yeah, I know." Matt rubbed the sleep out of his eyes and yawned again. "Hang on, I need a cup of java, be right back." As he disappeared down the hallway, Jacey drummed her fingers nervously on the couch and examined the room.

A bolt of orange silk hung from a hook just over the fireplace; it was gathered at the top, and it fanned all the way down to the floor. Jacey wondered if it were a souvenir from an exotic on-location movie shoot. An old club chair, a chipped coffee table, and two standing lamps with fringed shades were the only furniture; old wooden blinds covered the two windows facing the street.

Adding to the dark vibe was an array of unframed posters practically covering the stucco walls. Classic rock stars like Jim Morrison, Jimi Hendrix, and Janis Joplin hung next to movie posters of *Rebel Without a Cause*, Steve McQueen's *Bullitt*, and *The Godfather*. The most eye-catching poster featured a cherry-lipped girl sucking a lollipop: *Lolita*.

She did not notice any posters for any of Matt's movies.

Jacey had called Emilio from the car and browbeaten him for Matt's address, then followed the car's GPS system to a neighborhood called Los Feliz. Modest, one-story stucco homes, much like Matt's, lined the streets.

She soon smelled coffee brewing. A few minutes later Matt was back, holding a mug that said, WORLD'S BEST GRANDSON. He settled himself in the club chair across from her.

"I don't jump out of bed for just anyone," he teased. His eyes, just above the rim of the coffee cup, twinkled mischievously. "It's way early for me."

In other circumstances Jacey would have been amused, but she wasn't now. "This whole thing is nuts. And you know it! If anyone can step in and fix things, it's you."

"You're giving me a lot of credit," he said, sipping his coffee.

"Influence. You have influence—you've made these amazing movies, and you were the first one cast in *Dirt Nap*. You have some say over who your costar will be." She leaned forward on the edge of the couch.

He knitted his eyebrows together. "Not as much as you think."

"Come on, Matt—the producer's *daughter*? You care so much about this movie. Aren't you the tiniest bit freaked out that your costar got the role with no experience or auditions?"

"Of course I am. But are you really here to ask me if I'm bummed that it's not you?"

Her cheeks burned. "No, I'm just saying, you're the star of the movie. I know you can do something about it, Matt."

"Believe me, Dimples, if I could, I would. I honestly thought you nailed that audition. I mean . . ." He stared into his coffee, shaking his head slowly. "It was like you raised the level of the whole movie, right then and there. Made it better."

Jacey brightened. "I want to . . . I want to be as great as you are, Matt. Like when you asked if I wanted to be a starlet or an actor. I think you know my answer."

"Knowing what you want is crucial. But there's also the reality of working in this town. It's not like, you're the best plumber, you're gonna get the contract. In Hollywood, things are different—decisions are made on a whim, or because someone got bribed, or for a million reasons."

"What was the reason in this case? Why suddenly her over me?" Jacey asked pleadingly.

"It doesn't matter. Do you know what a producer does? He puts up money for the movie to get made. His money, his choice. Without him, there's no movie at all. Simple as that.

"Now you know exactly how Gina felt," Matt added. "She had that role in *Four Sisters*, and then due to stuff she had no control over, she lost it—the role that made *you* a star."

"Okay, fine, so the Karma Gods have spoken," Jacey threw her hands up in disgust. "Now, can I have my role back?"

Silence.

"Can't you at least go to bat for me?" she heard herself whimper. "I mean, if you were me, what would you do?"

"Trash a bar, probably. It's my rep. Maybe I'd live up to it for a change."

She scowled at him.

"Hey, you asked," he said. "Okay, seriously, I'd do what you're doing—try to wheedle my way back in."

"You think I'm wheedling?"

"Aren't you?" He pinned her with his eyes, alert, intense now. "If that didn't work, I'd let it go. Move on."

"To what?"

"Well, you're already working on a movie. Concentrate on that one."

"I don't understand," she said, feeling her chances of Matt's helping her slipping away.

"Is there anything you can do to make *Galaxy Rangers* a better movie? To turn the thing around, prove the buzz wrong?"

"How? I'm not the director, producer, writer. I'm just an actor."

"With an attitude like that, you're at the mercy of other people all the time. Look, Dimples, no one's ever gonna work harder for you than you are. Not your agent, your posse, your boyfriend—"

Ouch. That stung. Logan had barely reacted at all to the news that she'd either gotten or lost the movie.

"You gotta be proactive," Matt was saying. "If there's any way to make *Galaxy* better, find it, figure it out. 'Cause, you know what? Success is the best revenge. Show those jerks they were wrong to boot you from *Dirt Nap* because of bad buzz—if that was really the reason."

She hung her head. He wasn't even going to try to help.

Matt came over and sat close to her on the couch. He put his arms around her. "When I asked you why you were really here, I knew the answer—I just wanted you to be sure of it."

She sniffled as she looked up at him. His eyes were kind, his smile sincere. "You're here because you can disappear into a character: you can own her. You can make the whole world believe you are her—no matter who 'her' is. Do it with *Galaxy Rangers*."

"You really think I could do that?"

"Yeah, Jacey, I really do."

She was out-and-out sobbing now. "I'm not sure I'm that talented."

"Forget about talent. Acting isn't just a passion for you. It's how you breathe, it's your life."

She gazed up at him.

"Don't you get it? Baby, you never decided to be an actor. It's in you. Always was. Acting picked *you*. Do you really think you could *not* do this?"

"I'm scared," she admitted.

"We're all scared. We're actors."

Jacey turned, rested her wet cheek on his chest and let the tears flow freely. Matt held her close and stroked her hair. Jacey looked up at him, at his curvy lips, his intense eyes. She tilted her head up, closed her eyes, and gently pressed her lips upon his.

Matt did not return the kiss.

Jacey cupped the back of his head with her hands, ran her fingers through his hair, and pulled him closer. She applied more lip-pressure, then daringly parted his lips with her tongue.

Matt hesitated for a split second. Then he kissed her back, passionately. It was slow, sweet, and sexy.

And brief.

Matt hit the brakes. He pulled away and caught his breath. "If you're trying to bribe me to get you back on the movie, it won't work."

"I kissed you, Matt," she said quietly, lowering her gaze. "It had nothing to do with the movie."

His silence unnerved her. She dropped her hands from around his neck.

"I can't . . . we can't . . . this isn't going to happen, Jacey." Matt stood up.

"Why not?"

"I don't think of you that way. I don't feel . . . that . . . for you."

"I don't believe you."

"You should." He got up, went to the door, and opened it for her.

She paused, then walked out the door and to her car in a daze. *He gets me.* He gets me in a way Logan doesn't, in a way no one ever has. He gets why I'm here.

But he doesn't want me.

The realization struck her like a lightning bolt. She leaned over the steering wheel and sobbed.

jaceyfan blog

Jacey Double-dumped!
Got Tissues?

Jacey's so sad! Besides the public humiliation of being brutally booted from *Dirt Nap* (that indie she wanted so badly), looks like she's been kicked to the hometown curb, too. Sources say that Logan Finnerty, unhappy at the short shrift Jacey gave him at the prom, has cast his eye elsewhere for comfort and companionship. He's been awfully cozy with his prom queen, wannabe actress Tiffany West.

Too bad Jacey can't go crying to Matt *Can*-say-no! His rep for loving 'em and leaving 'em is well earned! Is it lonely falling from the top, Jacey?

Chapter Nineteen

The Rebound

Adam Pratt, devoted reader of all things Jacey, including the idiotic blog, spent the entire next morning trying to get a reaction out of her. He greeted her with "So I guess a prom appearance wasn't enough to keep your boyfriend after all."

"Sorry, I don't speak moron," Jacey retorted.

"Like I keep tellin' ya, Jacey, you need a guy in the industry. Who gets you," Adam yammered on. "You're out of Logan's league now. You've moved up, he's moved on."

"Outta the way, Adam, I've got a scene to shoot." She raised her chin, turned on her heel, and brushed past him.

Jacey was spectacular that day. Rage—deserved or not—at Adam, at Logan, at Matt, at the blog, at losing *Dirt Nap*, at the media circus her life had become, fueled her.

Today, she used it to get inside Zorina's skin. She nailed her lines, hit every mark, infused every scene with real emotion.

When they wrapped, Emory came bustling over, beaming. "That was massive, Jacey. They were right about you—you're phenomenal. When you want to be."

"Thanks, I think." She scrunched up her forehead.

Emory heaved a sigh and started to waddle away. Staring at his broad back, barely covered by his wrinkled shirt, Jacey felt a sudden stab of sympathy. He wasn't a bad guy, nor untalented. His big goof was probably picking the wrong movie for his directorial debut. That, and being so insecure he listened to Adam Pratt.

"Emory?" Impulsively, Jacey reached out and touched his elbow. "Any chance you wanna catch a bite?"

The director cocked his head as if he weren't sure he'd heard her correctly.

"I've never been to the commissary," Jacey said. "I hear it doesn't completely suck. Do you have time? We could talk about the movie."

"Uh . . . I guess." Emory appeared suspicious and grateful at the same time. Jacey had never reached out to him before. Why now?

Maybe, she thought, it would keep her from turning her cell phone on to see if Logan or Matt had called. Maybe it would keep her from having to discuss things with Dash, Desi, Ivy, Cinnamon, and Peyton, or keep her away from the newsstands, and from her Sidekick, where the story had probably spread, viruslike. Maybe it would keep her self-esteem from plunging any lower.

Okay, maybe there were selfish reasons. It didn't mean Emory wasn't appreciative.

The commissary was a cafeteria on the studio lot. Everyone working there, from crew members to studio execs, from lowly interns to the biggest movie stars, ate there.

She and Emory were shown to a small table for two by the window, where they ordered the commissary's famous Chinese chopped chicken salad (for her) and a thick, juicy burger (for him) and fries (for both of them).

It didn't take much prodding (by her) for Emory to confide, "I'm worried about the film, Jacey. Not your part—I'm lucky to have you."

She was touched. "What's worrying you? I mean, exactly."

"You haven't heard the buzz?"

"Everyone's heard the buzz, Emory. But that's all it is—words. You, of all people, shouldn't believe it. You're the director."

"The bloggerazzi are vicious, sinking us before we've finished filming," Emory said grimly. "I don't know where they're getting information, or why they're targeting us."

"Maybe you shouldn't read the blogs," suggested Jacey, who knew lots about *that* topic. "I heard that early gossip on *Titanic* was awful. People were saying it was going to be a box office disaster. And then it turned out to be the biggest movie ever."

Emory's rueful smile was heartbreaking. "Do you think *Galaxy Rangers* is our *Titanic*?"

Only in that it's sinking for real, she thought. Sinking under the weight of nonsensical plot holes so big you could steer the *Queen Mary* through them. Only in that it was character-challenged, lazy, clichéd—and those Adam-championed changes! Mind-blowing special effects, she supposed, might save it. Maybe. Possibly. Potentially.

Doubtfully.

So why had she chosen it? Light schedule, short shoot, big money. She'd been seduced by the money and taken the easy route.

"Don't think you'll look back on this as one of your better career moves." Emory echoed her thoughts. "I'm sorry."

"It's not your fault," she told him. "You didn't write it."

"Yet, as director, I take the bullet. That's how it works in this town."

Jacey put her fork down and considered. Was there any way, even at this late date, to make it better? Was there a way, as Matt had suggested, to be proactive, to save the movie? Emory listened to Adam—he might also be open to her ideas. If she had any.

So, what would make *Galaxy Rangers* more interesting to her, more appealing to audiences?

If you cared about the characters, you'd care about their plight. If you understood them, if they seemed like real people, you'd want to know what happened to them. You'd root for them.

"What if . . ." She measured her words carefully. ". . . We film some backstories, allow the audience to glimpse our characters growing up? Like, if we see Zorina as a child, with her parents, what values they instilled in her, how devoted she was to them. And if we explore young Zartagnan's relationship with his exacting father, Zaftiga's with her verbally abusive mom . . ."

"Go on," Emory said, warily.

Jacey continued. "We could just do quick-cut flashbacks, so the audience will understand the characters—and so the actors will, too. I think maybe we could all do a better job that way."

"What you're suggesting," Emory said, "could be brilliant. But . . ."—his shoulders sagged—"it means additional scenes and time to shoot them. We'd have to hire actors to portray the parents, and you guys as youngsters. It translates into more money, and extra time. We have neither."

Jacey wasn't ready to give up. She tried to picture *Galaxy Rangers* as a movie she and her friends would want to see. Then it hit her. "How 'bout we save money by cutting down on the special effects?"

"I don't follow," Emory said. "You're talking about adding scenes, not deleting them."

"I'm saying we won't need as many. Maybe we cut some of the not-so-great scenes and delete some scenes we haven't filmed yet. Substitute, not add." Jacey was really making this up now—she had no idea how much things cost.

"Writing new scenes costs money," Emory mused, stroking his stubbly chin, "unless . . ."

Slowly, he reached behind him, into the beat-up messenger bag that held his laptop. "I started in this business as a writer. Maybe I could do some script-doctoring."

"Would it be okay if I threw out some ideas?" Jacey asked, trying not to show how jazzed she was. Emory was listening to her, taking her seriously.

"Go for it," Emory said, powering up the computer.

"Well, the major twist is when Zaftiga turns out to be the one betraying them. But what if we went back and subtly planted a clue as to how each one in the group has something, some secret that could cause them to go to the dark side.

That way, when it's revealed, it'll be a real twist, not something the audience saw coming a hundred galaxies away."

Emory's round face lit up. "Yeah! Wait . . . let me get this down." He began typing away.

They lost track of time, sitting at the commissary and brainstorming. Emory wasn't on board with all of her ideas, but several sparked new, excellent ones of his own.

Jacey was juiced, and newly respectful of Emory Farber. For the first time during the entire *Galaxy Rangers* experience, she felt creative, funny, valued, and part of a real team. She was working on a story that, if the studio execs approved, would unfold on screen and be viewed by millions. Okay, maybe not millions. Thousands. Hundreds. Just her posse. Whatever. Now, she couldn't wait to re-create Zorina.

They stayed in the commissary until closing time. Before she and Emory were asked to leave, Jacey offered one final thought. The idea surprised him, but he promised to pass it on to the casting directors.

It was Jacey who suggested who should be cast to play Zaftiga's conflicted mom. The role was small—only two scenes—but pivotal.

That was how Gina Valentine ended up in *Galaxy Rangers*.

And how Jacey came to believe they were finally even.

jaceyfan blog

Who Am I?

When I started this Jaceyfan blog, even I didn't know how much fun it would be! Props to Jacey for giving it up. Who knew America's sweetheart, *Gen Next*'s beauty, wasn't so sweet after all? Between Jace and her posse, I could have written a complete tell-all book—oooh, good idea, maybe I will!

We've come to a fork in the road, Jacey fans. It's decision time. She has nothing lined up post-*Galaxy Rangers*. What will she do?

Hightail it back to Boring-field Hills, Michigan, and fight for what's rightfully hers—Logan—or stay in Hollywood and make things fun for me?

There are new rumblings about *Galaxy*

272

Rangers—that somehow, Emory Farber, with help from Adam Pratt, has performed lifesaving surgery on the script. And that, instead of the F/X-a-pa-*loser* people were expecting, this movie is actually going to be boffo! Box office gold. Which'll be more than just another notch in Jacey's belt—girlfriend has a sweet back-end deal. She stands to make millions!

So, what'll it be? Reclaim the boy back home, or move on, live the roller-coaster Hollywood life? Kick it old-school style, or kick old school to the curb?

P.S.: I started this blog four months ago, and neither Jacey nor her posse has a clue who I am. Damn, I'm good.

Chapter Twenty

Where Your Real Friends Are

"Are you going to call Logan back?" Desi asked delicately.

On Saturday afternoon, the group was lazing around their backyard pool, relaxing on the zero gravity ergonomic floating recliners Dash had bought—and pressing Jacey to communicate with Logan and find out if he were really dating Tiffany.

"All relationships go through ups and downs," Ivy counseled. "Just because the prom sucked, that's it? You guys are over, without even talking about it?"

Talk about it? Jacey wasn't sure she'd even know where to begin.

"Have you been ignoring his calls?" Dash intuited. "Usually you tell me everything, and I haven't heard a word about you guys since the prom. What's going on, Jacey?"

"I'm not sure, Dash." Jacey was on her back atop the aqua-toned, pillowy inflatable device, paddling around the pool slowly.

"Has she listened to his messages?" Desi asked Dash.

"She's giving him the cold shoulder? I didn't know that!"

"Maybe she doesn't know what to say to him," Desi mused. "I get that way sometimes. When it's all just . . . too big, too much."

"Or maybe she doesn't know how she really feels," opined Dash.

"Hello! I'm *here*!" Jacey chastised them. "Stop talking about me like I'm invisible."

But Dash was right. She *was* conflicted about Logan. Deep down, she'd been nervous about their relationship since the day she had won *Generation Next*—the day that had changed everything. Her life had taken off in a whole new direction, but they'd been so tight—she'd been so sure they could weather any changes, stay together through anything. Wasn't that what love was about?

She'd tried harder than he had.

She'd gone to the prom. He had not come to her premiere. She had been there cheering for him when he was crowned prom king, when he had led the basketball team to a winning season, when he had been made valedictorian.

Ooops . . . rewind. Not that last thing. She hadn't gone to graduation. Nor had Dash reminded her to congratulate him, send a gift showing her pride in him. Maybe that's why Logan was mad. If Logan *was* mad.

She hated the idea that Adam might be right, that there was no way a small-town boy could understand her anymore now that her life had changed so much.

"She should call him," Ivy said decisively. "They should talk it through. Lack of communication is what sinks a relationship."

"Suddenly you're the relationship expert?" Jacey paddled over to her cousin, and flipped her flotation device upside down. "I'd rather sink you!"

Ivy came bobbing back up to the surface and started to swim after Jacey, who held her palms up, as if surrendering. "Fine! *I'll* call him."

Before Ivy could dunk her, Jacey slid off the float, climbed out of the pool, threw a towel around herself, and headed upstairs to make the dreaded call.

Logan picked up right away. "Jacey! Finally! I've been trying to reach you."

"I know." She wasn't about to pretend she hadn't

gotten his messages. "I'm sorry, just been crazy busy."

"That's what I figured," he said.

"What's going on, Logan?" Jacey asked. "Are you with Tiffany now? Because if you are, I missed the part where you told me we were over." She hadn't intended to whimper.

"There was no part . . . You didn't miss it."

"So we're not over?" she said hopefully, holding her breath.

Silence.

"Logan? Are you there?"

"Jacey—it's just that you're so far away. Even when you came back for the prom, you were far away. Do you know what I mean?"

"No, not really. I got there late, but I was ready to spend the whole night with you, Logan. I was ready. If you know what *I* mean."

"Your timing sucks," he said quietly. "We were supposed to have the whole weekend."

"Let's not go back there, Logan. Just tell me, have you moved on? Are you and Tiffany, like . . . a couple?"

She didn't give him a chance to answer, because she suddenly wasn't ready to hear it. Instead, she babbled on. "If you've fallen for her, Logan, you should know, she's probably just using you. She wants to be famous. She gets with you—Jacey Chandliss's boyfriend!—*she* gets into the tabloids, she gets famous. Don't you see what she's doing?"

"Don't you see anything beyond yourself?" Logan retorted. "Not everything is about you."

"I didn't mean to make it sound like that," she whispered, stung.

"I don't *want* to break up with you, Jacey. I want you to come home. 'Cause everything would be different if you were here." Those last words seemed torn from him.

It'd be different, she thought dejectedly, if *I* were different. If I weren't me. That's what he's really saying.

Jacey threw herself into her work, into filming the newly rejiggered *Galaxy Rangers*. Which made her too tired even to think about Logan for the next few weeks, and too exhausted to feel sorry for herself.

Emory, bless his blubbery heart and soul, had miraculously gotten the studio bosses to agree to yet another round of changes. His enthusiasm about the characterizations —and about saving money on fewer special effects—had won them over. The director proved smart enough, this time, to share credit for the new brainstorms with the entire cast. That got everyone, including Adam Pratt, on his side, and psyched. No one came in to work quoting the blogs anymore. The vibe among the cast and crew was refreshed, reinvigorated, positive.

That also applied to new cast member Gina Valentine. Maybe she felt grateful; maybe she wanted to say something to Jacey; but barring a personality transplant, that wasn't going to happen. She didn't suddenly become all warm and fuzzy, remaining as huggable as a cactus. Gina showed her gratitude in a different way. She dived into her part and acted with all her heart (who knew?) and soul. She delivered a kick-ass performance. She invented a character, made it her own, and made her two pivotal scenes count.

Jacey thought a lot about Matt. It'd been weeks since she'd had any communication with him. She was over being hurt by his rejection, through beating herself up at the pathetic way she'd come on to him.

Jacey had stuff to tell him. Although he hadn't gone to bat for her with director Noel Langer, he'd done more: he had inspired her. He'd forced her to take action with her career, with her life—made her see that acting was not just something she was good at. It was who she was. And for just that knowledge, she owed him heartfelt thanks.

Jacey got her chance sooner than she expected. One day, she returned home from the set, and there in the driveway was his Viper with its telltale license plate.

She heard Matt and Desi in the game room, from the sounds of it deeply and loudly immersed in a raucous video game competition. She was about to sail into the room and join them, when something told her to hang back and just observe.

Matt and Desi's repartee had an easy rhythm to it, like volleying Ping-Pong balls—kidding around, laughing, nudging, competing. They were sitting next to each other on the couch, clutching joysticks and bumping each other in the elbows, shoulders, knees, anything to throw the other off his or her game.

Dark, intense Matt, wearing shorts and a T-shirt, was laughing; round-ringleted, chipmunk-cheeked Desi was egging him on. They looked less like international movie star and straight-outta-Hamtramck posse girl than brother and sister. There was no strain, nothing electric, no sexual tension in the air. Their body language spelled out the easy camaraderie of two people who'd been friends forever.

How had that happened? Jacey mused. Was it all because Matt had spent childhood summers in Desi's hometown? They bonded so instantly and tightly.

"How'd your granddad like the new car?" Desi asked him. "Has he gotten behind the wheel yet?"

"Finally. He's a stubborn old bird. I've been fighting

every step of the way. Getting him to accept it was almost as hard as when I bought him the house. Good thing he doesn't know about the furniture and the monthly bills. He thinks his pension is paying for everything. He'd croak if he found out otherwise."

"Like you'd be any different?" Desi challenged. "You wouldn't be too proud?"

"I would be. But we're family, right? Whoever's doing good helps the others. Like you're doing with your old lady."

Desi's eyes were glued to the video screen. "True. Most of what Jacey pays me goes to my gram and my brothers. I wish they'd take more. I mean, here I'm living in freakin' paradise! Sometimes I don't even believe it's real. Of course, I want them to experience a little of this."

"Like I said, there's nothin' more important than family."

"Like *I* said," Desi crowed, kicking him, "you're dead meat—I won! Again!"

"You distracted me," Matt cried accusingly. "That's why you won. Okay, fine! Two outta three. You game?"

Jacey stood frozen, gripping the railing and grinning broadly. Desi had found a true friend in Matt. Not everyone in Hollywood was out to get something. Some people were real. Two of them were right in front of her.

★ ★ ★

Jacey went upstairs to sit on her terrace. She began reading through the newest script changes as she sipped a bottle of Perrier.

Then she heard footsteps.

"How'd you know I was here?" she asked, twisting her
neck to greet Matt as he stepped out on to the terrace.

"Your aura," he joked. "It's so strong—I just followed it
up here."

"No, really."

"Really?" Matt strode toward her, then stopped to
perch on the waist-high brick wall that surrounded the
terrace. "To be completely honest? I didn't know you were
here. Desi and I were hangin', and I came to check out the
view. Who knows, maybe I'll snag a Beverly Hills address
myself."

"No, you won't."

"Bet?"

"Matt . . ." She paused and drew her knees to her chin,
partly to steady herself. Already she was nervous in his
presence. "I'm glad you're here. I've been meaning to call
you."

"You have?" He turned away from her and pressed his
palms on the wall, gazing down into the street.

"I wanted to thank you."

"For what?" he asked, his back still to her. "Not for kicking you out of my house that day, I guess. Which I've kinda been meaning to talk to you about."

Jacey braced herself, got up, and walked over to him. It was hard to be that close without her stomach fluttering and her pulse racing.

Calm down, she ordered herself. Don't let him go back to that day.

"I wanted to thank you for talking to me. Turns out you were right. Once I figured it out, what I really want, what I really . . . love . . . The decisions aren't that hard."

Wow. Had she just said that? She sounded way more sure of herself than she felt. Score! She *was* a good actress!

"S'good," Matt murmured. "I'm glad." He didn't continue, didn't pick up the thread of what he'd dropped a moment ago—about the day he'd rejected her advances. That, she surmised, was probably for the best.

"I have a confession."

Whoa! They'd both said that at exactly the same time! What were the chances?

Laughing, embarrassed, he put his pinkie in the air, and she crossed hers with his.

Hyperaware of how close their bodies were just then, Jacey started to sweat.

"You first," Matt directed. "You started, anyway."

"I got home earlier, and I saw you and Desi. I kind of eavesdropped. So I heard pretty much everything you said."

"So, you got your answer, then," Matt said nonchalantly. "Now you know where my money goes."

"I'm really sorry," she said, feeling beyond idiotic. "That was so none of my business. It's . . . I just didn't realize . . ."

"No worries, Dimples. It's no deep, dark secret, but I don't advertise it either. It's what I do. It's who I am. That's what I was trying to tell you, that day back at my house."

Jacey tensed.

"Here's the thing," Matt said. "I wasn't exactly honest the last time I saw you."

"Honest about what?" Jacey asked.

"It's just, man, where you were going; it's not a road I want to go down."

"What do you mean?" Jacey inched closer to him.

He stared at her.

"So, you actually . . . kind of . . . were attracted to me?" she asked.

"Jacey: meet the mirror," Matt said, without a trace of sarcasm. "What guy wouldn't be? You're smokin'."

"Then—?" She held her breath.

"Then a lot of things," Matt said. "I don't do commitment well. I would only hurt you."

She nodded, but she wasn't so sure she believed a word he said.

"Besides," Matt continued, as if he'd rehearsed, "you're not even eighteen. I'm twenty-one." Suddenly, he laughed softly. "Reminds me of that dopey song my grandpops used to sing, something like . . ." He began to warble softly. *"Come back, when you grow up, girl, you're still livin' in a paper-doll world. . . ."*

"Matt? Don't quit your day job." She nearly burst out laughing, but at that second, he took half a step toward her and pulled her into his arms. He tipped her chin up and kissed her. Slowly at first, sweetly tentative.

Jacey was too terrified to move a muscle.

Then, gently, he parted her lips with his tongue and began to kiss her more intensely, more passionately. Her body responded, and she began to kiss him back, matching him in slow, sweet intensity. It felt so good, so natural, so surreal. She was kissing a guy who wasn't Logan. She wasn't stretching on tip-toes to reach his lips. All she could think was, *we fit.* Matt began to stroke her hair; her knees turned to jelly, and she slipped right out of his arms.

Laughing, they separated. Matt stepped away, leaving her dazed, yet strangely satisfied. For now.

"I've got Cinnamon Jones for you." It was Kia, Cinn's cranky little assistant. "Hold on."

Cinnamon had called repeatedly. After everything that had happened, she wanted to find out what Jacey's plans were. Jacey had yet to be clear.

The end of *Galaxy Rangers* was nearing. And a funny, almost unheard-of thing had happened regarding the space spectacular. Bit by bit, slowly but surely, first tentatively then definitely, the buzz—the all-knowing, everyone-believing-it, holy buzz-o-meter—had flipped. It was looking as though Emory Farber and his cast would pull it off after all. No one outside the film knew exactly what the fixes had been, what strings had been pulled, but word was leaking out that the new scenes ruled.

Jacey's agent was once again inundated with scripts, offers, bribes, from those who wanted Jacey to star in their new movies.

"I need to know, Jacey," Cinnamon pressed, "are you leaving? Or will you stay? I can't hold these people off much longer. Everyone needs an answer. Especially me."

"So, we're staying." Those were the first words out of Dash's mouth when Jacey knocked on his bedroom door and came inside.

"Would you?" Jacey asked, coming up behind him and massaging his shoulders. "I mean, you don't have to. You've got school . . ." She trailed off.

Dash twirled around in his office chair to face her. "I've already withdrawn my acceptance to University of Michigan and put in an application to UCLA. It's right here, in Westwood. Bye-bye, Blue . . . Go, Bruins? I think."

She lit up. "And Aja? I mean . . . are you two . . .?"

Dash shrugged. "I don't know where that'll go, if it'll go. It's too soon to know. I grew up a lot this summer when you weren't looking, Jacey. It's been some education! Here's a secret: I knew I wasn't going back, no matter what you did. But as long as you're staying, you know you can count on me. As long as you want me."

"You got a calendar that goes to . . . oh, forever? 'Cause that's how long I'll want you in my life."

Jacey found Ivy in her room, on the phone. Playfully, she snatched it from Ivy's hand. "Hey, Emilio, wanna go out tonight?" Jacey asked.

Ivy looked at her quizzically.

Into the phone Jacey said, "We're celebrating. . . . No! I did not get a part in another movie. We're celebrating that. . . . I'm staying in California. And with you listening in, I'm hereby asking my cousin to stay with me. Maybe she'll get a promotion, even." Jacey paused. "What's her new title? I dunno. What should it be? Boss of Jacey? Okay, I'll take that under advisement."

Ivy's grin lit up her face. She grabbed the phone back. "It doesn't mean you're moving in! So don't get any big ideas, mister." Then she laughed and rolled over onto her back. Jacey kissed the top of Ivy's head and left the room.

Desi had painted her room pink. She was curled up on the window seat and already seemed to know what was on Jacey's mind.

"Yes—that's my answer," Desi said, unable to hide a megawatt grin. "You know I'd do anything for you."

"This is actually not so much for me—it's kinda for you." Jacey perched on the window seat next to her, forcing Desi to scoot over.

"For me?" Desi asked.

"I would like you to finish high school."

"Why?" Desi, who'd dropped out to go to work and help her family, asked. "I don't need a high school diploma. If I stick with you, I'm doing fine."

Jacey bit her lip. "It's important, Des. It's something you do for you. It's a milestone in your life, an accomplishment to be proud of. I missed my own graduation; I'd kinda like to be there for yours."

Big tears fell from Desi's perfectly round eyes as she

looked up at Jacey. She tried to speak, but nothing came out.

"Cool!" Jacey beamed. "We'll hire a tutor; you'll be done in no time!"

Desi leaned over, and for a small person, hugged her so hard Jacey thought she might never breathe again.

Suddenly, Ivy and Dash came dancing into Desi's room, doing a mean tango. And a positively cruel rendition of *"Hooray, hooray, hooray, for Hollywood!"*

Everyone Who's Anyone
A Starlet Novel

Chapter One

Doin' It Up Malibu Style!

What: It's a wrap! You are cordially invited to join Jacey
Chandliss and costars for a Splash-Down Party,
in honor of the completion of her newest movie,
Galaxy Rangers.
Where: The Polaroid Beach House, Malibu
When: August 5, cocktails at 5PM; last dance at . . . ??
Who'll Be There: Everyone who's anyone.
This means you!
BYO: bikini, beach towel, biceps, booty and boobs

Barefoot and bikinied, seventeen-year-old Jacey Chandliss scampered up a rocky rise in the dunes along Malibu
beach. The biggest party of the summer was in full force

just below her. She needed a moment to savor this amazing scene she was now officially part of.

Jacey tipped her chin skyward, and inhaled the salty ocean air. There was something healthy about the sea breeze, even as it played frizz-o-havoc with her thick copper-colored hair. She took off her D&G aviator shades and placed them, tiaralike, atop her head.

To her left, the wide expanse of the Pacific Ocean.

To her right, a three-story, pink stucco beach house sat on the sand. It was hers! Well, at least for the month of August; Jacey and her friends were livin' it up in a real-life Malibu McCrib.

How strange and surreal was that?

Wait, it gets better.

A *People* magazine–issue's worth of Sexiest Young Hollywood Stars were right under her nose, dancing, noshing, playing kickball, and mingling. They were the tan, the toned, the tabloid-bait—the celebrities known by their first names only. Like Lindsay and Zac and Mischa.

"A celebrity petting zoo," her friend Dash called it.

Dash Walker was the boy-next-door from back home in Michigan. He was Jacey's closest male friend, one of her three BFFs, who'd come out west with her to kick off her acting career. The other two were Desiree (Desi) Paczki and Jacey's twenty-one-year-old cousin, Ivy Langhorne. The posse, they jokingly called themselves. Starlet is what they called Jacey.

Dash, Desi, and Ivy were mixing it up at the Splash-Down Party, hobnobbing with the stars, plus everyone else who'd been part of Jacey's latest movie, *Galaxy Rangers*. Over a hundred people had shown up for the wrap party. Even the richest stars, she'd found out, couldn't resist free food, an open bar, and the chance to bask in the glory of being among their own: the young, hip, famous, and fabulous!

Most amazing of all? Every single celeb was here because Jacey Lyn Chandliss, a once ordinary wannabe actress from Bloomfield Hills, Michigan, had invited them. Put it this way: a year ago, the closest she'd ever come to the Hollywood star species was when she read about them. Now, thanks to winning TV's *Generation Next: The Search for America's Top Young Actor*—like *American Idol* for acting—she *was* them. A movie star!

Jacey felt tingly, sweetly light-headed. This party was like being in some deep, delicious dream-state, with a "DO NOT DISTURB" sign on her door.

"Earth to Jacey! Come in, Jacey!"

She spun, nearly losing her footing.

"What's it like on your planet?" A male voice teased.

Okay, how long had curly-haired Dash been standing there, wielding two frozen margaritas and a smile?

Jacey blushed. "I was taking a moment."

"A moment contemplating how lonely it is at the top?" Dash asked dramatically.

"Lonely?" She tossed her head regally, taking a drink from him. "*Shirley*, you jest!"

"Is *Shirley* here too?" Dash pretended to look around.

They burst out laughing, and clinked glasses.

Blue-eyed, whip-smart "Seth Cohen" look-alike Dash had taken to life on the "left coast" like Paris Hilton to a camera. Jacey still didn't get his record-breaking assimilation.

When had the former conservo-nerd morphed into an L.A. hipster? These days Dash was all aviator shades, skinny jeans, and snakeskin sandals. Only his "George Clooney 2008" T-shirt belied his true, that is, former self.

Everything in Los Angeles was so different from back home in Michigan. Out here the vibe was casual entitlement, the views, breathtaking, the values—twisted. To say the least.

"I came to escort you back to the hoi polloi, Mistress of Malibu. Your presence is requested," Dash announced.

"By who, specifically?" She hoped it was Matt Canseco, the actor-slash-person-of-most-interest to her.

"Not Matt. He's not here yet." Dash knew her so well!

"Then who?"

Dash's cell phone rang. She heard him confirming, "I've got her, Cinnamon. Yeah, I know he's on his way. We'll be right there."

Cinnamon was Cinnamon T. Jones, Jacey's agent. Jacey couldn't guess who "he" was.

Dash enlightened her. "It's the big Guy—as in Landsman. Currently en route to our party."

Jacey tensed. Guy Landsman was the head of the movie studio releasing *Galaxy Rangers*. Which made him Jacey's boss. Cinnamon had insisted on inviting him, assuring everyone that Guy Landsman was far too important to actually show up.

"What a buzz kill," Jacey mumbled, following Dash down the dunes. "Who needs the boss, probably in some stuffy suit, at a party?"

"Adjust your attitude, Princess Persnickety. Inside word says that Mr. Boss Guy is about to drop the F-bomb."

"When did you start speaking in tongues?" Jacey asked. "What's the F-bomb?"

"You'll see."

Back down on the beach, Jacey threaded her way around tossed towels, discarded flip-flops and designer totes. Their owners, those who weren't dancing, were busy massaging each other's egos—gushing, hugging, back-slapping, tossing flowing tresses, and flexing muscled biceps.

Ice clinked in their glasses, and in some cases, through their veins. True, everyone here was a "someone," but not everyone was to be trusted.

Acknowledgments

Big ups to my East and West Coast friends for making this book possible, and accurate. Thanks go to: Helen Perelman, my first "roommate," who became a crackerjack editor and now, writer; Jennifer Besser and Brenda Bowen at Hyperion for creatively nurturing the series along; Phyllis Wender for support along the way; and Karen Miller for introducing me to Susan Kovinsky, who introduced me to Katie Zucker, who supplied many cool L.A. details.

If I left anyone out, let me know and I'll catch ya in book two: *Everyone Who's Anyone*.

And always, I am grateful to all the family and friends who put up with me, and encourage me.

And a shout-out to the pets who more than once scampered across the keyboard, nearly hitting the delete key. They know who they are.

Randi Reisfeld is the author of a number of young adult and middle-grade fiction books, including the T*Witches series—on which the highly rated Disney Channel movies are based—plus *Summer Share: Partiers Preferred*; *Oh, Baby*; and *Hooking Up*. Randi is the former editorial director of the teen monthly *16 Magazine*. The Starlet series draws heavily from her lifelong obsession with all things Hollywood.